Elizabeth Sarah Villa-Real Gooch

The Contrast

A Novel

Elizabeth Sarah Villa-Real Gooch

The Contrast   ·
A Novel

ISBN/EAN: 9783337000691

Printed in Europe, USA, Canada, Australia, Japan

Cover: Foto ©Andreas Hilbeck / pixelio.de

More available books at **www.hansebooks.com**

THE

CONTRAST:

A NOVEL.

BY

E. S. VILLA-REAL GOOCH.

·THE FIRST AMERICAN EDITION.

WILMINGTON:

Printed and fold by JOSEPH JOHNSON

No. 73 Market-ftreet Oppofite the BANK.

1796.

THE

CONTRAST:

A NOVEL.

CHAP. I.

ON the coaſt of Cornwall is a ſmall village, ſituate on a riſing hill, which
commands a view of the ſea. A chapel, built
on the ſummit, is its principal edifice; thither did the hearts of its humble inhabitants
repair to invoke the mercy of their Creator,
and oft did they implore him to protect ſuch
of their friends and relations as were expoſ-
ed to the boiſterous element below it. Nor
was this the only purpoſe to which this ſim-
ple building was adapted; frequently did its
white front borrow aid from the moon, and

ſerved as a land mark to the diſtreſſed mariu-
ers, who were driven within its view.

 This village, which I ſhall call Birtland,
might have been juſtly deſcribed as ſecluded
from the world. No proud lord uſurped its
happy domain. No legal plunderer attended
to ſettle thoſe trifling differences between man
and man, which, without ſuch interference,
might be ſoon adjuſted ; but which, when applied, frequently proves worſe than the evil.
At Birtland, the age of primitive innocence
ſtill exiſted ; at Birtland, all was union and
perfect tranquillity.

 Within two miles of this happy village ſtood
an ancient caſtle, formerly the reſidence of the
houſe of Haſtings. Many were the illuſtrious
Earls of Huntingdon who had drawn their firſt
and laſt breath of life within its then peaceful
walls. Every heir of that diſtinguiſhed title
had ſignalized himſelf by deeds of unbounded
munificence. They were as remarkable for
their benevolence and hoſpitality, as the cour-
tiers of the preſent age are for their arrogance
and boundleſs ambition. At THEIR door, never was the tale of woe rejected, nor did a
petitioner crave in vain. The wealthy and the
indigent were equally unknown ; and the
hearts and purſes of theſe noble lords were
ever open to the tears of the unhappy. To
obtain their protection, it was neceſſary only to
ſolicit it ; for no guileful wanderer ever bent
his way to the happy but retired caſtle of Ledſtone.

Many centuries had paffed in this ftate of blifs, when time, which is ever working miracles, (hitherto fatal to mankind !) ftretched the cloud of fate over this humble corner of England. The *laft* Earl of Huntingdon *died*. His generofity had over-reached his power, and his eftates were involved. That of Ledftone was an object of too much importance to be abandoned by the rapacious creditors ; it was therefore agreed that it fhould be put up to fale, and parted with by public auction.

A gentleman, the fon of a wealthy merchant in the city, was the higheft bidder, and to him was that property configned. He was a young man, not poffeffed of very fhining abilities, who had been educated at Weftminfter-fchool, and was thence fent to Oxford. But ftudy was ill adapted to his tafte ; he left both thefe places in difguft, and prevailed (but not without difficulty) on his father, to fuffer him to pafs two or three years on the continent, by way of giving a finifh to his education.

It was foon after his return to England, that he determined to marry, but he had frequently the mortification to find his propofals rejected. Money was no object to him, as he was fure to inherit, on the death of his father, a confiderable fortune ; but he wifhed to ennoble his name, hitherto beft known upon 'Change, and was at lenght fortunate enough to fucceed in his addreffes, with the only daughter of a newcreated Irifh peer, who had been fuccefsful in his claim to the title of his anceftors, and whofe greateft advantage was her title.

A 3

It was foon after this marriage took place, that he became the purchafer of Ledltone, which he knew only by report, having never vifited the Weft of England.' In London, Lady Jane was equally a ftranger. She had paffed her life in Dublin but remained unnoticed there until her father was created an Earl. They fet out for London too foon afterwards for her to fix her choice among her old acquaintance, who were many of them at length become her new admirers.

Mr. James Martindale was the firft monied man who folicited the hand of Lady Jane ; and to his fortune, more than to himfelf, was fhe immediately devoted.

CHAP II.

MR. Martindale hired a ready-furnifhed houfe in the vicinity of Portman-Square ; and on the fourth of June, juft five weeks after her marriage, Lady Jane Martindale was prefented at St. James's. Her perfon was rather handfome than otherwife, and it was on this occafion decorated with all the paraphernalia of birth-day magnificence. To be admired, it was neceffary only that fhe fhould be feen ; and to her, the knee of adulation was foon bent. The Earl of C———, on whom the fetters of matrimony fat lightly, was her devoted flave for the evening ; and her eyes received an additional portion of brillianty, as her conquefts became multiplied.

In Mr. Martindale's bofom very different were the fenfations which arofe on that occafion. He gazed on the beauties of his wife, and his vanity was flattered by their effect , but his heart trembled as he viewed her, and the pangs of jealoufy racked his foul. He endeavoured to appear regardlefs of the admiration he faw lavifhed on her ; but by degrees he drew nearer to the door of the antechamber, and their waited with anxiety the hour of twelve, at which time his fervants and equipage were ordered to attend.

As foon as their arrival was announced, Mr. Martindale hurried Lady Jane out of the room, and attempted to put on her cloak, which a footman had given into his hands. But Lord C————difputed with him this office, and the rules of good breeding obliged the hufband to relinquifh it. Yet he could not avoid perceiving a fignificant look, and a fqueeze of the hand, which each beftowed on the other, as Lord C————Handed Lady Jane to her carriage ; and this was, to a weak mind, almoft proof pofirive of their guilt. But in this idea he was wholly miftaken : Lord C————had not entertained an idea beyond the amufement of the prefent hour, and Lady Jane faw nothing in the emaciated peer that could poffibly turn her thoughts towards him on the fucceeding one.

The time now arrived when every faſhiona-
ble family prepared to leave town.   Lady Jane
had already made the acquiſition of numberleſs
acquaintance, but her heart had not ſelected a
friend.   It was almoſt a matter of indifference
to her whether ſhe went, and to her huſband's
inclinations ſhe appeared willing to accede.

Mr. Martindale's determination was to go to
Ledſtone ; but when ſhe heard of its ſecluſion,
her heart recoiled at the idea, and ſhe requeſted his approbation of a prior excurſion to Wey-
mouth or Brighthelmſtone.   He became however abſolute in his intentions ; and as her father
had immediately after her marriage returned to
Ireland, it became neceſſary for her to draw
ſome one over to her intereſts ; neceſſity, rather than choice, directed her to old Mr. Martindale.   He was exactly calculated for ſuch
an employment.   He had been in his younger
days a general admirer of pretty women, and
the charms of his new daughter-in-law loſt nothing in his opinion.   He perfectly agreed
with her, that to tranſplant a large eſtabliſh-
ment into the deſerts of Cornwall, would be
attended with a heavy expence, beſides the
probability that exiſted of their diſliking the
ſituation, and ſpeedily returning.   Lady Jane
and the old gentleman had many converſations
on the ſubject, and agreed to expoſtulate warmly with Mr. Martindale, whom however they
had the mortification to find *inexorable.*   All
they could obtain was a few days delay, and a
promiſe that their ſtay in the country ſhould
not exceed ſix months.

A NOVEL: 9

CHAP. III.

IN a few days, part of Mr. Martindale's re-
tinue set forward on their journey into the
West. These consisted of her Ladyship's un-
derwoman, who was, during this summer
campaign, to act also in the capacity of house-
keeper ;—a French valet ;—a French cook ;—
a running footman, and three or four more.
Every thing was there in readiness for the
reception of these nobel and novel guests; for
the castle was inhabited by an old steward and
his family, whom the late Earl of Huntingdon
had stationed in it ; and as they had never received notice to quit the premisses, they still
enjoyed, in some of the rooms at the end of it,
peacable and quite possession.

When these imitators of greatness passed
through the village of Birtland, they were
struck with the appearance of its humble inhabitants; who, mistaking them for their super-
iors, crowded forth to bid them welcome. The
bells, though few in number, echoed these
warm plaudits of the heart ; and every tenant,
with uplifted eyes, prayed Heaven to bless
them !

Stunned with applauses for which they were
unprepared, and which they did not rightly

comprehend, they anfwered only by a loud
laugh ; and arriving at the caftle, where they
foon made themfelves known, were received
with humble civility by the worthy fteward
his wife, and daughter.

Mrs. Drapery could not help fhuddering as
fhe paffed through the fpacious hall, which led
to the inhabited part of the caftle. The mafty
door clofed with a tremendous noife ; it re-
founded through the vaulted roof, and petrified
her with horror. On the high arched windows of painted glafs, were handed down to
pofterity the emblazoned arms of the newly
expired title of Huntingdon ; and the unwieldy
armour which had formerly defended the lives
of its illuftrious wearers, now hanging up and
neglected, borrowed a faint light from the
feeble glimmerings of the moon, fcarcely feen
enough to be obferved through the heavy
cafement.

She requefted to be fhewn to the apartment
allotted her, where fhe gave orders that her
fellow-tarvellers fhould attend. She expreffed
to them the greateft difguft at every thing fhe
faw, and the utter impoffibility there was of
her being ever able to accuftom herfelf among
fuch Hottentots. " She was fure," fhe faid,
" that all Mr. Martindale's money would be
" but a poor compenfation, if Lady Jane was
" to linger away the beft part of her life in fuch
" an odious retirement. She wondered how
" he could think of bringing an Earl's daugh-
" ter to fuch a horrible diftance from every

" thing alive. For HER part, fhe was fure
" SHE could not ftay there, and fhe hoped to
" find that her Lady would foon be of the
" fame opinion."

In lefs than a week, Lady Jane and Mr.
Martindale arrived at Ledftone. When the
loquacious Mrs. Drapery faw the butler (to
whom fhe was by do means averfe), fhe affured
him, that if fhe had not been certain of HIS
coming down, fhe could not have prevailed on
herfelf to remain there a day after fhe had delivered up her charge to her Lady; for that the
place was a defert, and the evening winds
were fo rough, that fhe already found her con-
ftitution DAMAGED by them; and it was become abfolutely neceffary for her to return to
London, were it only for the benefit of her
health.

Lady Jane and Mr. Martindale, who faw
nothing in their new habitation otherwife than
they had expected to find it, paffed feveral days
in vifiting the caftle and its environs. Lady
Jane was particularly attentive to the narations
of the old fteward, who not unfrequently rub-
bed his hand acrofs his eyes, as he dwelt on the
praifes of his late-loved Lord. In a fmall clo-
fet adjoining the hall, of which he had entreated to keep the key, he was wont to review and
admire the tattered robes in which Henry third
Earl of Huntingdon fat in judgment on the trial
of the charming and unfortunate Mary Queen
of Scots. Thefe he fhewed Lady Jane, lamenting forely the day, that, in depriving the

county of its FIRST ornament, robbed HIM of his beft friend—HIS ONLY BENEFACTOR.

CHAP. IV.

THE mind of Lady Jane was by nature fufceptible of tender fentiments, and of foft impreffions; yet her heart was as unconfcious of their primitive fource, as of their fubfequent confequence; and fhe had hitherto beheld every one with general indifference. She however poffeffed an immoderate degree of pride and oftentation, and was emulous to out-vie all who dared afpire to equality with her; affuming a forbidding air of loftinefs, which often offended the focieties fhe lived in. But, over-ruled at length by the recollection of the more exemplary conduct of fome of the amiable part of her female acquaintance in London, and elfewhere, fhe in fome meafure conquered that difagreeable HAUTEUR; and the tender and growing impulfe of nature beginning to infpire her with ideas more confonant to the texture of her difpofition, fhe became thoughtful, and rather melancholy; deriving her chief pleafure from wandering in unfrequented paths, and exploring and forcing tracks through the mazy and moft intricate parts of the foreft, which lay at a fmall diftance from the park.

In one of thefe folitary perambulations, chance had directed her fteps to the ruins of a very ancient, and once capacious tower, fituate on the fumit of a ftupendious cliff. Thence fhe could obferve, with the help of a fmall telefcope which fhe carried in her pocket, the various objects which the ocean continually prefented to her view, and which with their novelty and variety together, became every day more pleafing and interefting to her fancy.

Mr. Martindale rofe one morning early in the month of September, before his ufual hour, to take the diverfion of fhooting; his gamekeeper having apprized him the preceding evening of a covey of partridges which frequented a wheat-ftubble near a pleafure-ground adjoining the park; not that Mr. Martindale difcovered any more eujoyment in the purfuit of rural pleafures, than did his lady; but his time hanging rather heavy on his hands, and as fhe did not permit him to beguile any part of it in affociating with thofe whom her own choice had not approved, and pointed out as proper companions for him, he was obliged to feek amufement in queft of pleafures which nature had not given him either tafte or inclination to enjoy.

Lady Jane had rifen at her ufual hour, and was preparing for breakfaft, when Mr. Martindale tired of his vifionary fcheme of pleafure, returned heartily fatigued in the purfuit of it.

The moment they had enjoyed their early repaft, Lady Jane with eager fteps precipitate

B

ly bent her way to her much-favoured spot; which she had no sooner ascended, than she instantly discovered through her glass a small boat making for the shore; and excited by curiosity, she advanced with deliberate attention down the sandy beach, towards the edge of the water. As the boat approached nearer her view, she thought she perceived in it five persons, together with some casks which they had stowed, and piled up in a regular pyramid, in the stern of their little bark. The tide having recently laved, and now retired from, its beachy limits, had caused the sand under foot to be exceedingly wet; and what would have wonderfully terrified Lady Jane at any other time, and on any other occasion, now stimulated her boldly to venture on; and she walked, or rather waded, almost knee-deep in the briny ocean, till she came within reach of the floating objects which she had first discovered; but having left her glass within the tower, she could scarcely distinguish of what sex or age the persons were, until they approached nearer.

They were soon securely landed in a place where she had not been accustomed to meet with human beings (she having dedicated this deserted spot to solitude, and her own reflections); and the unexpected sight our mariners experienced of a beautiful and elegant female, who seemed to be lost in astonishment, could not fail to excite in them an equal degree of surprise. After some little conversation, they requested to be informed of the nearest town, or village; having come, they faid, on fhore for the purpofe of procuring freſh water for their veffel, a fmall brig, bound from Green-ock to London, which lay at anchor at the dif-tance of about two leagues.

The perſon who chiefly addreſſed himſelf to Lady Jane, appeared to be a military man, a-bout fifty years of age. He had a complacency of manner which indicated the gentleman; his countenance beaming that ineffable fweetneſs which generally befpeaks the mind at eafe. This gentleman introduced to her his friend who accompanied him (the other three were failors, bufily employed in laſhing the boat to the remains of what had formerly been a light-houfe.) The drefs of the latter, who was ma-ny years younger, denoted him a Highlander; and the gracefulnefs of his mein inſtantly caught the attention of Lady Jane. She invited them both to the caſtle, and promiſed to fend fer-vants thence to render their men and boat e-very affiſtance their fituation required.

This propofal they thankfully accepted; and inwardly congratulated themfelves on the no-vel and ſtrange adventure with which chance had fo far favoured them.

ON their arrival at the caftle refrefhments
of every kind were by Lady Jane's order
fet before her guefts. She enquired for Mr.
Martindale, but was informed by the butler
that he was gone out on horfeback, and had
left orders to tell her ladyfhip that he fhould return to dinner by five. She apologized for his
abfence, and entreated them to relinquifh
all idea of going back to their veffel with the
evening's tide; obferving, that the days were
now fhort and clouded—the nights long and
dark; and fhe farther alleged, that their ignorance of the coaft might lead them into unavoidable difficulties, and imminent dangers,
which fhe would by no means advife them to
encounter, and which would diminifh with the
return of day-light. She inwardly wifhed (but
from what caufe fhe knew not) that Mr. Martindale fhould fee them, and approve what fhe
had done. She felt eager to juftify her conduct to him, perhaps from a confcioufnefs of
felf-created uneafinefs fhe had never before experienced. Her fluttering heart beat high with
a defire of fhe knew not what; and her faltering tongue feemed almoft deprived of utterance,
as her eye, involuntarily and conftantly met
thofe of the young and accomplifhed Caledoni-
an. She wifhed, fhe faid, to detain them till

Mr. Martndale's return; and even when he did return, fhe feared the day would be too far fpent for them to hazard with fafety the attempt of regaining their fhip :—fhe at laft hinted to the elder gentleman, who feemed anxious to depart, the kind of impropriety there would be in their going away without feeing him. This objection had fufficient force, to counter-balance, in their minds, every other.

Having drawn from them a promife-fhe too ardently wifhed, fhe requefted their attendance in the park and gardens, whither they cheerfully confented to accompany her. In one of the walks fhe perceived by accident that her drefs had materially fuffered from her excurfion on the fands; fhe then left her vifitors to the care of the gardener, whom fhe directed to point out to them every object worthy their attention, and proceeded to the caftle to change her clothes; defiring the gardener to re-conduct the gentlemen there, as foon as their curiofity had been fufficiently gratified.

On her lapyfhip's return fhe retired to her appartment, and ordered her woman's attendance there. The article of drefs, which had been neglected fince her feclufion in the country, as a matter of indifference, now became an object of importance. Mrs. Drapery was one of thofe accommodating abigails who are ever ready to flatter and encourage the-follies and vices of their employers, and fhe neglected nothing on the prefent occafion to adorn the perfon of her lady; fignificantly adding,

" With what pleafure her mafter would be-
" hold her ladyfhip at his return home, look-,
" ing once more LIKE HERSELF !"

Before the etiquette of drefs was finally ad-
jufted, Mr. Martindale entered the room fome-.
what abruptly ; having been informed by the
fervants of his new vifitors, and wifhing, previous to his feeing them, to know of Lady Jane
who they were, and what were the motives
that had thus induced them to take up their refidence in his houfe.

Lady Jane briefly related to her hufband each
circumftance ; contenting herfelf with obferving, that although fhe had not enquired their
names, fhe was fure, from the little fhe had
feen of them, that they were perfons of no inferior rank : fhe juftly remarked that the laws
of hofpitality were of themfelves fufficient to
juftify the hafty zeal with which fhe had preffed them to wait his return.   Mr. Martindale
coincided with her opinion, and left her to do
honour to his guefts.

As foon as he was gone, Mrs. Drapery,
finding herfelf emboldened by her lady's vifible
embarraffment (which together with the attention to her drefs had not efcaped her), begged
pardon for informing her ladyfhip, that fhe.
knew perfectly well who the gentlemen were,
having enquired of the failors, who had fatisfied her in every refpect.   They were both, fhe
faid, Scots.   The old gentleman, whofe name
was *Stuart*, had been many years Colonel of

the *Mountaineers;* but had retired from the
fervice about two years. His lady was lately
dead, and the lofs of her had taken fuch an e-
effect on his mind, that he had refolved to tra-
vel; and a fea voyage had been particularly
recommended to him, as being the moft likely
to recruit both his fpirits and his health. The
young gentleman. whofe name was *Glencairn,*
was diftantly related to the deceafed Mrs. Stuart, who had one only child, a daughter, now
educating in a convent at Calais. She was to
come over on their arrival in London, and to
return with them. Mrs. Drapery indeed FAN-
CIED, but it was only her own conjecture,
that the Colonel had thoughts of uniting the
young couple; as the young gentleman had no
other reafon for coming over, than that of
keeping the Colonel company; and of returning with him to Scotland, as foon as Mifs Stuart fhould have joined them.

Lady Jane was not fo regardlefs as fhe appeared to be of the information given by her
officious waiting-woman. She, however, af-
fumed an air of compofure fhe was doomed never more to feel, and with hafty fteps joined
the gentlemen below.

COLONEL Stuart had been in the mean time equally communicative to Mr. Martindale ; he had confidered it as incumbent on him to introduce himfelf and friend to his acquaintance. Mr. Martindale, foon after Lady Jane's appearance, retired to his dreffing-room, whence he fent to requeft her attendance for a few minutes ; when he informed her, that fhe was not miftaken in the favourable opinion fhe had entertained of the ftrangers ; and proceeded to tell her all with which Colonel Stuart had made him acquainted. She did not think it neceffary to mention to him the cenverfation fhe had held with her maid ; but pretended to liften with curiofity to what he related ; which differed in nothing more than his filence on the fubject of Mifs Stuart, who fhe naturally concluded had not been mentioned.

Lady Jane returned to the faloon, where fhe furprifed Glencairn drawing founds of fweeteft melody from Mr. Martindale's flute, which lay on the table. He laid it down when fhe appeared, but by her defire took it up again, and played once more, at Colonel Stuart's requeft,

I wifh I was where Helen lies !

in a manner fo peculiarly his own, that Lady Jane, for the firft time in her life, felt the power of mufic over a fufceptible mind. She was at that moment alive to the moft tender fenfations ; her foul vibrated to the touch, and fhe felt a pang of exquifite enthufiafm.

——He ceafed ;—and her eyes more ex-preffive than her tongue, folicited his continu-ance. He fmiled confent, and then play-ed

Abfence ne'er fhall alter me.

The words funk deep into her heart ; her fine eyes gliftened ;—and fhe had but juft time to turn them on Colonel Stuart, as Mr. Martin-dale entered the room.

The converfation became general, and din-ner was announced. It was a domeftic party, and Lady Jane being without a female friend, had no excufe to leave the room when it was over. Mr. Martindale and the Colonel enter-ed into a long converfation ; and the old war-rior-feeming for a moment to forget his griefs, gloried as he recounted his former exploits.

Tea, and lefs interefting airs on the flute beguiled the remainder of the evening ; and an early fupper was ordered, as our vifitors were under the neceffity of departing by day-break. Lady Jane gave orders that coffee fhould be prepared for them, and after an hour or two paffed in focial delight, they reciprocally bade adieu.

The Colonel expreſſed to Mr. Martindale his wiſh of meeting with him in town; but ſaid that as he might not be appriſed of the time when the Ledſtone family arrived there; and as he was ignorant alſo in what part of it he ſhould fix his ſhort abode, he begged of Mr-Martindale to take the trouble to enquire after him at the Ducheſs of G———'s in St. Jame's Square, who would be able to aſcertain whether he ſtill remained an inhabitant of London, or was returned (which was more likely) to the ſequeſtered mountains of Scotland.

Lady Jane had no ſooner retired into her dreſſing-room, than ſhe gave orders to Mrs. Drapery (who, as I before obſerved, now acted in the double capacity of her woman and houſe-keeper) to riſe at a very early hour, that nothing might be wanting to complete the elegant hoſpitality the ſtrangers had experienced at Ledſtone. She retired to bed, but did ſhe retire to reſt?—Ah, no!—The image of Glencairn was before her; ſhe pretended drowſineſs, and in ſecret ſilence wept her cares to ſleep. Mr. Martindale, fatigued by the exerciſe and events of the day, and unconſcious of the thorns of diſcontent which invincible Love had ſtrewed over his wife's pillow,

Snor'd out the watch of night.

Lady Jane liſtened at day break, but ſhe heard nothing. All was huſhed in profound ſilence. They had departed an hour before their appointed time: but they had not eſcaped the anxious vigilance of Mrs. Drapery; who fearful of offending her lady by not feeing them, and fearful alfo, of her own weaknefs fhould fhe trull herfelf to fleep, had prevailed on her friend the butler to pafs the intermediate time with her in the houfe-keeper's room, over a comfortable bottle of madeira, which he was to provide from the cellar as foon as the family was retired to reft.

Mrs. Drapery, though a keen woman, was by no means deftitute of female weaknefs : fhe repofed an implicit confidence in the butler, and at once informed him of her fufpicions relative to her lady, and the young gentleman ; who (fhe muft obferve) was of a figure to captivate any lady's heart. She did not know (or had not fenfe enough to find out) that Mr. Oldfon, the butler, was warmly in his mafter's intereft; not from any rafh confidence *that* hitherto infenfible mafter had repofed in him, but from a fenfe of the lucrative place he enjoyed. Mr. Oldfon therefore made few comments on her obfervations, but treafured up in his mind every circumftance that might lead hereafter to a farther afcendancy over Mr. Martindale ; as he had already prevailed on him in many trivial occurrences, which had turned out in the end to his own advantage.

Soon after the bottle of madeira was exhaufted, Mrs. Drapery told him fhe heard a noife ; but fhe fuppofed it to be too early for the ftrangers to be thinking of their departure. She however liftened, and heard it repeated ;

it was, she said, the sound of feet gently mo-
ving down the great stair-cale. Mr. Oldfon
liftened, but heard nothing. Mrs. Drapery
still perfifted that she DID hear a noife ; and as
she had encouraged the idea of ghofts haunting
the caftle, she requefted Mr. Oldfon to accompany her up the ftair-cafe leading from her
room ; at the top of which they faw our five
travellers ready to depart. Mrs. Drapery's
eyes inftantly fixed on thofe of Glencairn ; who
anfweredthem by a fign that he had fomething
to communicate. It was eafy for her to turn
Mr. Oldfon's attention to the other, while she
privately received from his hands a guinea, and
a flip of paper carefully folded and fealed.
Thefe she immediately conveyed to her pocket,
while Mr. Oldfon was making his bow to the
Colonel, in acknowledgement of what he had
from a very different motive conveyed to
him.

Mrs. Drapery and Mr. Oldfon faw the travellers depart, and then retired to their refpective rooms. The former cautioufly placed
her pockets under her head, as fearful that her
fecret fhould be difcovered, and by that means
the confidence of her lady be loft for ever.

C H A P. VII.

IT was not difficult for Mrs. Drapery to underſtand the uſe it was intended ſhe ſhould make of both the objects ſhe had received ; yet ſhe was not ſufficiently miſtreſs of her lady's thoughts to hazard a forward avowal of her conduct in receiving them. When ſhe attended Lady Jane in the morning, ſhe could not avoid perceiving that ſhe had been in tears ; and ſhe preſumed to enquire with evident ſymptoms of affection, *if her ladyſhip was unwell ?* At this unexpected queſtion, Lady Jane gave vent to her full heart, and ſtrove not to conceal her emotion. She imprudently leaned on her woman's boſom, and, in apparent agony, aſked whether the gentlemen were gone, and if ſhe had ſeen them ? Mrs. Drapery told her that they were ; and that ſhe had attended them according to her ladyſhip's order. She drew by degrees the letter out of her pocket, and entreated her ladyſhip's pardon for the liberty ſhe took in offering it to her peruſal. She aſſured her that ſhe had no time to return it after it had been put into her hands ; and that pity for the poor young gentleman's ſorrow at his departure had afterwards induced her to ſecrete it, until ſhe might ſee him again.

C

Lady Jane took the letter with feeming re-
luctance, and found it to contain the following
words :

" Be not offended, Madam, at the prefump-
" tion of a ftranger, who till he faw you,
" never dreamt of love.   His profound refpect
" for your name and character will condemn
" him to mifery and future filence ; and he
" would not have hazarded this liberty, had he
" not read in your eyes an expreffion of ten-
" dernefs which they have too furely, and
" probably too fatally, conveyed to the def-
" ponding heart of
                                   "EDWARD GLENCAIRN."

    Lady Jane trembled as fhe read the letter,
which fhe immediately conveyed into her pocket, and Mrs. Drapery delighted in the fuccefs
of her undertaking ; for although fhe felt that
cuftom, and the laws of decency, would require that fhe fhould maintain her place as a
fervile dependant, fhe from this moment confidered herfelf the bofom friend of her lady ; and
exulting in what had paffed, began to fuppofe
herfelf the appointed and convenient confidante
of every future action of her life.
    From this unhappy period, fhe began to ex-
ert the influence fhe had obtained over the
mind of her hitherto fpotlefs lady ; and avail-
ing herfelf of a advantage common to low
minds, did not fail NOW AND THEN to remind
her, by a gentle hint, that fhe was in her
power. Lady Jane's youth, and ignorance of
the world, induced her to be filent where fhe
might have been allowed to complain ; but

her timid foul as apprehenfive of the injurious
conftruction her hufband might put on the adventure, and fhe refolved to fuffer in filence.
She had no wifh. no intention to deceive him ;
yet fhe fighed as fhe reflected on the merits
of Glencairn, whom fhe defpaired of feeing
more.

We will now return to our mariners. They
had a tedious and rather perilous paffage to
London, where they landed in three weeks.
Colonel Stuart's firft care was to difpatch a
meffenger to a mercantile houfe in the city,
whether his letters were addreffed. He received one from Mifs Stuart, earneftly requefting him to go to her. She informed him that
her health had been for fome months gradually
declining ; but that fhe had hitherto avoided
mentioning that circumftance to him, waiting
till fhe heard of his arrival in London ; allcdg-
ing, that fhe was fufficiently acquainted with
his feelings, to be convinced that had he
known her fituation fooner, he would have
haftened his journey from Scotland, probably
to the prejudice both of his health and conven-
ience.

Colonel Stuart had not feen his daughter
fince her mother's death, as fhe had been near
four years at Calais. He fpoke of her feldom;
but his thoughts often dwelt with rapture on
the idea of once more folding his treafure to
his heart, and retracing in her growing features the refemblance of his loft and lamented
wife ! Alas ! what were the fenfations he ex-

C 2

perienced at the perufal of her fatal letter! It was a deep ftab to his wounded mind, and it became neceffary for him to call religion and reafon to his aid, to prevent him from immediately finking under the weight of it.

All that friendfhip could fuggeft—all that the moft tender fympathy could invent, were on this trying occafion warmly exerted by the amiable Glencairn towards his unhappy friend. He urged the poffibility of Mifs Stuart's being too eafily alarmed about herfelf; that the melancholy infeparable from a monaftic life had probably induced her to give way to ideas which derived their principle origin from her feclufion;—that the moft effectual means to be employed towards promoting her recovery, were to amufe her mind; which had fcarcely began to unfold itfelf, ere the event of her mother's death, and her father's fubfequent correfpondence, ftamped an impreffion on it, that time, and a more fuitable way of life, would be (in *his* opinion) alone capable to efface.

The voice of confolation infenfibly gained upon the Colonel; his misfortunes grew lighter as he liftened to the advice of his friend; his heart in a few hours recovered in fome meafure its former ferenity; and inftead of wafting time in deploring the evil that threatened him, he endeavoured to avert it by haftening to join and cherifh her, who, fince the death of his wife, feemed doubly entitled to his care and protection.

NOTHING material occurred during their journey to Calais ; but Glencairn, to whom every object was new, was surprised at the different scenes that presented themselves. Often, however, did his imagination retrace the image of Lady Jane Martindale ; she was the first woman he had ever beheld with emotion, and her expressive looks had taught him to believe that he was not indifferent to her. He lamented both the cause and its effect, that had, by preventing their continuing in London, deprived him of being presented at the Duchess of G————'s, where he could obtain the only chance of the Colonel's hearing of, or seeing Mr. Martindale. But these reflections he was obliged to conceal ; they remained with his secret buried in his heart- and he was under too many obligations to the Colonel not to endeavour (at least) to suppress them.

When they landed at Calais, and had reached Monsiur Dessin's hotel there, Colonel Stuart found himself fatigued and agitated by his journey. He requested Glencairn to go immediately to the convent, with a note from him to the superior, desiring her to send Miss Stuart, with the bearer, his friend. Glencairn had formerly seen her ; but it was dur-

ing thofe days of infancy on either fide, that
had left but few traces behind them. He delivered his letter at the gate of the convent,
and was conducted to the parlour, on one
fide of which, was a large grate ; and on
the other fide, a curtain that was drawn.
In a few minutes it was removed, and prefented to his view a form that nature had tak-
en pride in adorning.

Mifs Stuart (for it was herfelf) was the
moft finifhed picture of human perfection. She
raifed her blue eyes as he addreffed her, and
politely requefting him to wait a few minutes,
difappeared to put herfelf in readinefs to accompany him.

She foon rejoined him in the parlour, and
they proceeded on foot to the hotel. She accepted his arm, and he perceived with extreme forrow that fhe had fcarcely fufficient
ftrength to proceed. Yet fhe did not once
complain, but paffed the fhort time in making
a thoufand tender enquiries about her father.

The meeting between them was highly affecting ; they were equally fenfible of the
changes each other's looks had experienced,
yet neither dared to acknowledge that they
perceived any alteration. It was but too evident that Mifs Stuart was in the early ftage of
a confumption, which appeared to be faft haftening this beauteous bloffom to a premature
decay. It was foon determined that fhe fhould
immediately leave the convent ; that the next
morning her expences fhould be paid there;

and her clothes taken away; and that they
ſhould allow themſelves a few days repoſe at
Calais, before they fixed on any plan their
inclinations might for the preſent lead them
to purſue.

Miſs Stuart had contracted an intimacy in
the convent with a Miſs Beaumont, a young
lady of French extraction, and ſomewhat older than herſelf. The very ſlender fortune ſhe
was to inherit, had induced her parents tô perſuade her to take the veil, to which ſhe was
perfectly reconciled. Having lived in the convent ſince ſhe was ſix years old, ſhe had not a
wiſh to ſee the world, but had partly reſolved
to enter on her noviciate the following year.j

Miſs Stuart called there the next morning,
and took leave of her friend. They agreed to
correſpond during the remainder of their lives,
and that no intereſting circumſtance ſhould occur to the one, with which the other ſhould
not become acquainted.

Our travellers had been near a week at
Calais, and Colonel Stuart thought it time to
fix their departure. But whither were they to
go? He wiſhed, for his own gratification, to
return home; but he thought it would be, at
that time, a wrong meaſure to adopt on his
daughter's account. For this he had a double-
motive: Winter was ſetting in, and he naturally conceived that the keen blaſts of the
North would have too powerful an influence
over her delicate and affected frame. He feared

alfo, from the exquifite fenfibility he preceived
her to poffefs, that fhe might receive a fatal
blow to her peace, when, on her return to
her firft home, every object which appeared
there would remind her of its loft ornament,
her mother !—The Colonel had, fince her
death, found a melancholy pleafure in arrang-
ing every thing at Allan-Bank for her reception.
All that had belonged to Mrs. Suart, he had
collected carefully for her daughter; but he
had no idea of the faded form he was to meet;
he had feen her a healthy, though delicate girl;
and he naturally expected to find in her im-
proved underftanding, and formerly lively difpofition, the companion beft fuited to footh the
anguifh of his mind, whenever he reflected on
the virtues of that incomparable wife of which
the grave had robbed him !

   In the evening, when Mifs Stuart had retired
to her appartment, the Colonel rang for ano-
bottle of Monfieur Deffin's beft Burgundy, and
imparted to Glencairn his reflections of the day.
He obferved, that having nothing to confult
but their refpective inclinations, he had entertained an idea of their traveling South ; that
he thought his beloved Mary's health required
change of air, and he conceived it poffible
THAT of Italy might reftore it. She would alfo
derive many advantages from fuch a TOUR,
that were not to be met with in Scotland. It
would afford her a fine opportunity of improving herfelf in mufic, of which fhe was paffionately fond; and fhe would by travelling gain a
fufficient knowledge of the world, to conquer

that awkward bafhfulnefs, which gave her a childifh air of fimplicity, and which it would be neceffary for her to overcome before fhe prefided at his houfe, of which, alas! fhe was now become fole miftrefs. Glencairn could not with any propriety appear to difapprove this fcheme, and nothing remained but to obtain Mifs Stuart's approbation (of which they could have no doubt); and that obtained, they refolved to quit Calais, and pafs through Provence to Nice.

Mifs Stuart was, as they expected, pleafed with the propofal; and nothing was wanting to complete the fatisfaction of the party, but a more cheerful acquiefcence on the part of Glencairn, who vainly endeavoured to forget his predilection for Lady Jane Martindale. He experienced an inquietude hitherto unknown to him, when he reflected on the impoffibility there now was of his communicating to her his fentiments, and the knowledge of his fituation. He dared not hazard writing to her by the poft; and though the failors had told him Mrs. Drapery's name, his refpect and delicacy forbade his addreffing himfelf to her. He was forced therefore for the prefent to relinquifh all hope of feeing, hearing of, or writing to her; and he felt the force of Rochefoucault's juft obfervation, that

Abfence leffens fmall paffions, and encreafes great ones.

For he never loved Lady Jane fo PASSION-

ATELY as at this moment, while he defpaired of ever feeing her more,

CHAP IX.

THE next day was employed in preparations for their departure; and on the enfuing morning they began their journey in a berline the Colonel had purchaced of Monfieur Deffin. They were attended only by a French fervant who had travelled all his life, fpoke a little Englifh, and whom Deffin had recommended.

I fhall pafs over every natural incident that occurred to them, and obferve only that they reached Nice foon after the time they had calculated to do fo ; when, after paffing a few days at the hotel, they hired by the month an elegant villa in its environs.

The Colonel had procured letters of credit on the Englifh banker there, and they were all alike charmed with their new fituation. Their fervant Louis had been there frequently, and was become their *Proveditore-Generale.* Mifs Stuart hired a maid for herfelf, by name Jofephine, which, with an Italian cook, compleated their family.

Colonel Stuart was an independent, though

not a rich man. His income had never been involved, and it produced him from five to fix hundred pounds a year. He had no one to provide for but his daughter.

With his protégé Glencairn it was otherwife. He was an orphan, without a friend in the world but the Colonel, who (having been many years intimate with his deceafed father, diftantly related to Mrs. Stuart, and who was a younger brother of high birth, whofe fortune perifhed with his life) had adopted this *child of love*, and promifed never to defert him. He adhered to his word, and was fufficiently prepoffeffed in favour of his young ward, to WISH that a future attachment might take place between him and his daughter, that his fortune might by their marriage equally devolve on both. With this view, he had fpared no pains to cultivate the mind of the young Edward, who repaid his tender care with all that filial duty and fincere affection could beftow.

It was with this young couple, as with all our untravelled iflanders, whofe extent of European knowledge carries them no father than the boundaries of England; every object beyond Dover becoming a matter of wonder. Thus it was with our North Britons. Mifs Stuart and Glencairn were loft in aftonifhment at every new fcene which prefented itfelf to their view, and they feemed to fancy themfelves inhabitants of another world. They were left almoft entirely to themfelves; for Colonel Stuart was a man of fuch ftrict honour, and had

withal fo much family-pride, that he believed
it impoffible they fhould derogate from either;
his only apprehenfion was, that neither poffeffed fufficient confidence to explain thofe mutual
fentiments which he thought muft be infeparable from both. In this opinion he was not al-
together miftaken. Their time paffed away in
innocent delight; and Mifs Stuart's health beginning vifibly to mend, they amufed themfelves in vifiting every curiofity, with which
the charming country they were now become
inhabitants of, abounded.

In the vicinity of Nice, innumerable were
the picturefque fcenes which met their ravifh-
ed eyes. How beautiful do the maritime Alps
appear, as they rife from the ocean! from
whence afcending by gentle degrees, they form
a fuperb amphitheatre, bounded by Mount-
albano, projecting into the fea, and over hanging the town. On the other fide, where pro-
fpects lefs ftupendous allure the eye, how
charming do the richly cultivated plains appear, while they prefent to the view the vines,
the citrons, the oranges, the bergamots, and
every luxury which Earth can furnifh to her
inhabitants!—The gardens, which are during
the winter months equally profufe of the
fweeteft flowers, convinced them, that in that
terreftrial paradife the Lord of all had been
peculiarly bounteous, and that to be happy it
was neceffary only to forget every difappointment that had hitherto awaited them in this
fublunary world.

But how vain is every endeavour to command the feelings of the human heart!—They rife fuperior to controul, and if they reign at all, they reign with tyranny. Glencairn muft have been more than mortal, lefs than man, could he have refided under the fame roof with the all fafcinating Mary, without feeling the power of her improving charms. He was not blind to them, but often in fecrecy lamented his wayward deftiny, which feemed determined in fpite of every oppofition to feparate them through life. An idea, prior to his feeing Mary, had taken full poffeffion of him. He had beheld Lady Jane Martindale, and his heart had vowed to her everlafting love. He even cherifhed the certainty of her hufband's not being IMMORTAL; and he conceived it poffible for a time to arrive, nay, he even believ'd it to be not far diftant, when he might return to England, and claim her as his own.

How vifionary is every fcheme of future blifs, and how precarious are the wifhes of man!—He builds his hope on a fhadow; and fcarcely has he time to admire the fabric his imagination has raifed, ere it vanifhes, and his dream of happinefs at once difappears!

WE will now return to Ledſtone, where
nothing material occured during the
ſummer and autumn months, more than has
been mentioned. Lady Jane and Mr. Mar.-
tindale lived peaceably together, ſeldom con-
tradicting each other, but particularly agree-
ing on one point, that of looking forward
with pleaſure to the deſtined time of their return to London. Lady Jane ſometimes, indeed, recollected Glencairn; but thoſe emoti-
ons ſhe had experienced at firſt ſeeing him, had
ſubſided into a' languid indifference, and her
thoughts became every day more devoted to
the idea of the pleaſures ſhe ſhould enjoy in
the gay metropolis. She did not however neglect at times viſiting her favourite ſpot; but
it was now winter, and the coldneſs of the
weather prevented her ſitting there as formerly, watching the boſom of the deep.

She was one morning returning from it,
and near the houſe, when ſhe perceived Mr.
Martindale coming towards her with a letter
in his hand. His countenance bore the viſible
marks of diſcontent. He took her arm within
his ; and ſlightly obſerving that he had ſome-
thing unpleaſant to communicate, but without
mentioning of what nature, they proceeded
to the library, where, without hiſitation. he

read to her the letter. It was from his father. It first contained a few vague enquiries after them, and then informed them, that being at length tired of a single life, he had resolved to marry a second time. He had partly, he said, fixed his choice. The Lady (he observed) was not of a distinguished family, neither did she possess a brilliant fortune; but she had many good qualities, and he had no doubt of the approbation she would meet with from his son and daughter, to whom he hoped in a few months to introduce her as his wife. He neither mentioned her name, her age, nor her person; and of these, various were the opinions they entertained. Mr. Martindale highly respected his father, and dreaded seeing him the dupe of what he naturally supposed to be (from the caution observed in the letter) an indiscreet engagement. Another motive too, and in some breasts it would have been a more powerful one than it was in that of Mr. Martindale, was *self-interest*. The old gentleman had, on the death of his wife, settled all his landed property on his son; but he had a great deal of ready money; five thousand pounds of which he had given him on his marriage, besides his mother's jointure of two thousand pounds a year, which was, in case of Lady Jane's surviving him, to be her portion for life. He had been indeed particularly liberal on that occasion, having presented Lady Jane with the late Mrs. Martindale's jewels, which were of considerable value, and he had purchased every thing for them, such as equipages, plate, &c.

It was impossible they could forefee with pleafure an union which would divide, if it did not wholly alienate, the affections of Mr. Martindale from his family. After they had confulted together for fome time on the fubject, they agreed to fet out for London with all convenient expedition. Mr. Martindale anfwered his father's letter, but in terms almoft as equivocal as his own. He expreffed fome furprife at the half confidence repofed in him, and concluded by wifhing him every happinefs in whatever fituation he might hereafter find himfelf; but he did not give the moft diftant hint of his intention of going to town, which was in hopes, if it were not already too late, to fruftrate the old gentleman's prefent intentions.

As they had no houfe there, they were on their arrival obliged to put up at an hotel; and had on that account left all their fervants, excepting Mrs. Drapery and the butler, at Ledfione. They had not been there many minutes, before Mr. Martindale fent for a hackney-coach, and went to his father's houfe in the city. But how great was his aftonifhment, when, on knocking at the door, a footman in an unknown livery appeared at it, and informmed him, that the houfe was now in poffeffion of another family ; Mr. Martindale having been married about a month, and that he refided in Devonfhire Place !

Mr. Martindale fmothered as much as poffible his indignation and furprife. He directed

the coachman to return to the hotel, and gave
himfelf up to his reflections in this firft inftance
of duplicity on his father; for it was evident to
him, that he was actually married at the time
he wrote to him ; and that the ceremony muft
have been performed in a very private manner,
not a fingle news-paper having announced
it.

When he returned to Lady Jane, and informed her what had paffed, he had the fatif-
faction to find that her feelings were perfectly
congenial with his own : fhe perfuaded him to
wait till the next day for farther intelligence ;
and amidft a thoufand conjectures—apprehenfions—and uncertainties—they paffed the evening, and retired early to reft.

C H A P.   XI.

MR. James Martindale, at a feafonable
hour, difpatched his own fervant with
a dutiful, yet cool billet of congratulation to
his father, requefting to know at what, hour
he might be premitted to wait on him.

Though it was but juft two o'clock when the
valet was fent on his errand; he found the
crowd of fervants and carriages fo great at Mr.
Martindale's door, that it had more the appear-

ance of the Exhibition at Somerfet-Houfe, than of belonding to a citizen.

, It was fome minutes before he could prevail on one of the footmen to carry up the note he was intrufted with. After waiting a confiderable time for an anfwer, a verbal one was brought him by another powdered coxcomb, which was fimply Mr. Martindale's compliments, and that he would call at the hotel within an hour. Lady Jane was ftanding at one of the windows of it about four o'clock, when a fumptuous vis-a-vis ftopped at the door. Mr. Martindale was fitting by the fire-fide, reading a new pamphlet, when Lady Jane's precipitate exclamation, of " Good " God ! this cannot be your father !" inftantly drew him towards her. They thought they recognized his features, though difguifed under a fmall wig, made to look like his own hair; which gave fo great an alteration to his countenance, that it was impoffible for them at the firft moment to afcertain whether or no it was really him they faw. They were however foon convinced, as he hobbled out of his carriage fupported by two fervants in yellow and filver liveries : the plain blue and buff, which had been the family ftandard of many years, was to all appearance difcarded, with the brown bob of former and more refpectable days.

Mr. Martindale received the congratulations of his fon and daughter with much feeming pleafure ; and apologized with rather a difconcerted air for the fecrecy he had obferved towards

them; alledging as his reafon for it, the apprehenfions he had entertained for their difap-
proveing his marriage; to which however he
was very certain no reafonable objection could
be ftated, unlefs it was that of a difparity of
years; Mrs. Martindale being extreamly
young, and extreamly handfome. He was
commiffioned by her, he faid, to fay a thoufand
kind things to them both; and to affure them
of her regret at finding herfelf engaged not
only for that day, but for the fucceeding one;
but fhe hoped they would not refufe her the
favour of their company to fupper that night
at twelve, after the opera, where fhe was going.
To this they affented, more from curiofity
than inclination, and the old bridegroom took
his leave.

Mr. Martindale, in going down the ftair-
cafe with his father, enquired the former name
of his mother-in-law; but received a very
laconic anfwer, that it was *Harvey;* of a family of the North of England, with which he
could not poffibly be acquainted.

He returned, and fat down in fullen filence;
but Lady Jane laughed. She had no envy in
her compofition, and was prepared to admire
the fuperior beauties of Mrs. Martindale, without a wifh to outvie them, or to find them
any way inferior to the old gentleman's dif-
cription.

At the appointed hour they went to De-
vonfhire-Place. Mrs. Martindale was but juft

returned home, having lounged, she said, longer than she intended in the saloon of the opera-
house.

If her visitors were struck with the beauty
of her person (than which nothing could be
more captivating), they were not less so with
the dazzling splendour of her dress, A rich
gold muslin, made into a Circassian robe, with
a turban of white crape, ornamented with a
profusion of diamonds, gave her the appearance of an eastern princess; but there was an
air of levity in her manner, that instantly caught
the attention of young Mr. Martindale; who
had scarcely beheld her, ere his heart formed a
wish that no violent intimacy might in future
take place between her and his wife.

The more he saw of this youthful bride
(whose appearance did not bespeak her age to
be more than seventeen), the less he liked her;
and while he drew her into a conversation, in
which he perceived that her ignorance and
self-sufficiency were predominant, he pleased
himself on the comparison he could not avoid
making between her, and the less beautiful,
but more lovely and unadorned Lady Jane;
who having, since the small portion of knowledge she had obtained of her heart, lost a considerable share of that pride which had ever
been her greatest foible, was become infinitely
more interesting to society, and more amiable
in the eyes of her husband. In HER was blend-
ed all that increasing sensibility could bestow
on an intelligent mind. Polite without flatte-

ry, she every day gained on the esteem of those who knew her. Mrs. Martindale, by endeavouring to appear the woman of fashion, for which she was never intended, was at times even vulgar ; and her obscure origin was not counterbalanced by the graces of her mind. Nature had been, it is true, profusely lavish on her person ; but her disposition was avaricious and mean. She disliked Lady Jane's superior birth, but she had cunning to dissemble ; and endeavoured to flatter her into a belief, that she had never seen any woman with whom she so much longed to cultivate a friendship, as herself.

We will now take leave of this family party for the night ; they parted, not without a voluntary offer from Mrs, Martindale to break off all acquaintance with those of her society whom Lady Jane might not approve. I will next inform my readers who was Mrs. Martindale ; which, together with the little sketch I have drawn of her disposition, will in some measure enable them to account for the tenor of her future conduct ; at least, if they think as I do, that a low mind never attains any degree of excellence, however the person may be exalted. The heart when *good* is incorruptible, however the mind may be overuled by the force of custom and of example : but when both these are bad, the stain is indelible, and can never be expunged.

MRS. Martindale was one of the many children of a refpectable tradefman in Newcaftle, and on a vifit to her elder fifter, married to a corn-factor in the city, when Mr. Martindale firft faw her. He foon became enamoured ; for his heart was not fufficiently frozen by age, to be able to withftand the renovating influence of youth and beauty. The idea, however, of marrying her, or any other woman, did not once occur to him. The fifter, who was artful and defigning, perceived his inclinations, and determined to turn his weaknefs to the advantage of her family. She invited, or rather forced him into all their parties ; and finding, after a few weeks, that he did not make any overtures towards her fifter's eftablifhment, fhe told him with much apparent concern, that fhe found her fifter's character had fuffered materially from his conftant attendance on her ; that fhe had loft by it a very eligible marriage ; the gentleman (who was a young officer) having withdrawn his addreffes in confequence of it, and that it was become neceffary for him to difclofe his intentions, of whatever nature they might be.

This was a trial for which the old gentleman

was not prepared. He hesitated, as undeter-
mined what to answer; till on being told that
there was no alternative between his marrying
Miss Harvey, or seeing her no more, he was
weak enough to wipe the tears from his eyes,
and in half-broken sentences, extorted by FEAR,
as well as LOVE, he promised to offer her his
hand. In less than half an hour he had con-
sented to fall into the snare that was laid for h-
him. The family desired the engagement
might be kept secret, in order to avoid, they
said, the ill-natured sarcasms and reflections the
world would cast upon his age: but the truth
was, they dreaded the advice of all his REAL
FRIENDS, and hurried him into a promise of
hasty marriage, without allowing him time to
consider what he had to expect from its future
consequences.

Having been thus prevailed on without difficulty, he thought of nothing but his intended
bride. He was profuse in his presents to her;
and on her mentioning that she thought the city air inimical to her health, he dispatched an
agent, of her sister's recommending, in pursuit
of a house at the west end of the town. This
trusty and well-chosen ambassador made choice
of the one in Devonshire-Place; and so exactly
did he answer the confidence reposed in him,
that he actually made, in Mr. Martindale's
name, an agreement for the purchase of it; so
that no farther trouble was imposed on the old
gentleman, than to sign the bonds which were
two days afterwards put into his hands. It is
true that he once accompanied the ladies to

look at it; but was there a fault that he could
poffibly find with a houfe fit for the reception
of any nobleman's family? Could any houfe
be too good for Mifs Harvey? Could any ex-
penditure that lay within the compafs of Mr.
Martindale's drafts, be extravagant?

The furniture of his houfe in the city was to
be the next confideration. There was not e-
nough of it, neither was it fufficiently modern
to be tranfplanted into Devonfhire Place. The
moft fafhionable upholfterer in town was therefore immediately applied to, and directed to
change it as his fancy directed. He was to be
allowed one thoufand pounds, over and above
the value of what he took from the city; and
of which he, as the moft fafhionable, and con-
fequently the moft confcientious tradefman,
was to be fole appraifer. That furniture was
not, as I obferved, fuited to the prefent tafte,
but it was coftly in the extreme; and was e-
qually good, though not equally ornamental,
in the inferior as in the beft apartments. The
late Mrs. Martindale's dreffing-room was fitted
up in the moft expenfive manner; innumerable were the rich ornaments it contained; the
beautiful inlaid and Indian cabinets, the tall
mandarians, and fine China jars, were not the
moft remarkable. The boxes belonging to her
toilette were, like thofe of the rich, but nar-
row-minded Lady S———, of filver inlaid
with rubies; the bird-cages were of filver wire,
and every article difplayed *grandeur*, if not
(according to modern ideas *elegance*. Some of
thefe Mifs Harvey wifhed to preferve; till a

gentle hint from her fifter reminded her, that
as they had been the property of the late Mrs.
Martindale, who had doubtlefs fet a value on
them beyond their intrinfic worth, it was probable that, if they were in *her* poffeffion, her
fon might wifh to obtain them for Lady Jane
to keep in remembrance of her. Nothing
therefore was to be given into his hands, but a
large portrait of his mother, with which he
was to be favoured on his return to town ; Mifs
Harvey MODESTLY obferving, that, confcious
of her own unworthinefs, fhe fhould fear a rival in that picture whenever Mr. Martindale
looked at it, as he would naturally draw a com-
parifon between his two wives, which could not
fail to be an unfortunate one to herfelf.

The houfe was foon ready ; the jewels, wed-
ding clothes, and equipages, foon bought ; and
nothing remained but to fix the happy day,
which foon arrived. But the one previous to
it was marked by a little event, which it may
not be unneceffary to mention in the next chap-
ter.

E

CHAP XIII.

ON the morning preceding the day that was to make Mr. Martindale the happiest or moſt miſerable of men, he perceived that an unuſual gloom overſpread the fine countenance of his deſtined bride. He preſſed her hand to his lips, and entreated to be informed of the cauſe. She burſt into tears, and ſuddenly withdrew, leaving him and her ſiſter together.

From HER, he anxiouſly prayed to know the meaning of ſo ſudden, ſo alarming a change; tenderly enquiring if he had left any thing undone by which it was poſſible for him to prove ſtill farther the extent of his affection. The emotion too viſible on every feature of his face, and the eagerneſs with which he conjured her to explain in what he had offended, forced at length, from this TENDER relation, the avowal of a converſation her ſiſter had held with her; which amounted to nothing nore than a childiſh idea that had entered her head; a kind of fear, that if ſhe was wretched enough to ſurvive Mr. Martindale, his ſon, unmindful of his father's tenderneſs might diveſt her of all his goodneſs had laviſhed on her. He might poſſibly in the end turn her out of her houſe, and take poſſeſſion of it,

as his heir. It was not (fhe was very fure)
from any mercenary motive that her fister had
encouraged this thought; it was that of a young
girl fund of magnificence as a child of a new toy,
and like that, fearful of loofing it. This was
a fufficient hint for the too generous and too
credulous Mr. Martindale; he fent immediately for his attorney; and gave him inftructi-
ons to draw up a marriage fettlement, by which
he gave her the houfe in Devonfhire Place,
with all its appendages; together with all the
ready money he fhould die poffeffed of, ftocks,
dividends, &c. &c. &c. allotting only one
thoufand pounds of it as a legacy to Mr. Martindale, or Lady Jane if fhe furvived him;
his landed property having been, as I before
faid, already fettled on his fon.

In a few hours all was figned, fealed, and
delivered; and he expreffed his gratitude at being told how to remove the imaginary grief
that had for a moment been fuffered to prey on
HER, to whofe happinefs he was determined to
devote the remainder of his exiftence.

The next morning the fun fhone refplende nt
on the nuptials of Mr. Martindale. They were fo-
lemnized as agreed on in a private manner;
and in the evening he conducted his bride to
HER OWN houfe in Devonfhire Place.

They had been there about a month, when
Lady Jane and Mr. Martindale arrived in town.
Mrs. Martindale had already formed the ac-
quaintance of almoft every fafhionable family

there. For, as I have read in scripture, *Wherever the honey is, there will the flies be also*, so is an open house, a sumptuous equipage, and all the other appendages of wealth, the sure passport to an intimacy with the whole world. Innate virtue is no recommendation; nor is any other requisite necessary to support the appearance of it, than the acquiescence of a husband to the conduct of his wife. However his delicacy may be wounded—however his feelings may be hurt by her failings—let him but continue to live with her in a routine of extravagant dissipation, and the feeble voice of slander will be drowned in the loud plaudits of the world. But, if he forsakes her, though she be " as chaste as ice, as pure as snow," she shall not escape the torrent of calumny, which will inevitably overwhelm her reputation. A woman's fame depends less on her own character, than it does on that of her husband. If he discards her, the world will also, without enquiring why he has done so.— She will look for friends, but she will never find them. The gay companions of youthful pleasures will shrink from distress, as from a pestilence; and she will woefully experience, that the fine day, *Flattery*, will not stay to assist the weary in a cloudy night. Alas! HER day will soon set in darkness—her breaking heart will be overwhelmed by the storms of adversity, until in some obscure corner of the earth she dies unknown—unpitied—and unlamented!

C H A P. XIV

MR S. Martindale foon gained a complete afcendancy over her doting hufband, which was ftrengthened by her apparent attachment to Lady Jane, who continued to be fo great a favourite with him, that her fanction feemed neceffary to every thing fhe undertook. She had art enough to twift herfelf round the heart of that lady, who repofed in her an unlimited confidence, and they became infeparable. They met with univerfal admiration; but their manners were fo different, that the admirer of the one was feldom that of the other. Mrs. Martindale's beauty and levity attracted the notice of all the gay men, while Lady Jane's increafing fenfibility gave her an air of *froideur*, that forbade them every hope of encouragement.

Mr. Martindale, fenior, though extravagant in the gratification of his wife's pleafures, was not wholly unmindful of his fon's interefts. He purchafed a fmall houfe for him in Argyle Street, to which he was prompted by his wife

Lady Jane believed her to be only the artlefs, giddy girl fhe appeared. Little did fhe

E 3

suspect the snake she was fostering in her bo-
som, which waited only with envenomed ran-
cour to sting her beyond the reach of human
remedies.

Among the crowd of fluctuating admirers
that paid their devotions at the shrine of beauty,
Lord Darnley was the most conspicuous for his
attentions to Mrs. Martindale. He was lately
married to a very young lady, whose large
fortune had been in part appropriated to the
payment of his lordship's early debts. He was
fond of his wife, yet not sufficiently so to lay
any embargo on his inclinations whenever they
led him to indulge a momentary caprice.

He considered Mrs. Martindale an easy con-
quest, which, when once obtained, would be
soon forgotten. With this view he laid close
siege to her at every public place she frequented.; nor did she give his lordship any reason to
doubt the success of his enterprise. Vanity
was her ruling passion,_and to that she was e-
ver ready to sacrifice every moral considerati-
on. Lady Jane either did not, or would not
perceive this growing intimacy ; she conceived
Mrs. Martindale's levity to be her best security
against any attachment of the heart, and she
felt no alarms on her account.

'Lord Darnley was rather an elegant than a
handsome man. Perfectly versed in every les-
son of LOVE, he had seldom met with a denial
where he had once taken the pains to ingra-
tiate himself. He was at this time busily em-

ployed in raising a regiment of light dragoons for the service of his country ; and a desire of rendering himself conspicuous according with his notions of patriotism, he spared no expence to complete it. Seldom a day passed in which his emissaries did not inveigle new victims to satiate the rapacious thirst of ruthless war ! His lordship, equally a candidate for the fields of Mars and of Venus, divided his time between both. His morning hours were devoted to the misery and ruin of many poor and worthy families ; his evening ones to the more pleasing amusement of endeavouring to seduce the affections of any woman, to whom he might wish for the moment to render himself agreeable. Not that I mean to infer, that Lord Darnley was a bad man, he was only a fashionable one. Nursed in the lap of luxury by a most indulgent mother, his earliest wishes had not been left ungratified. He had been returned from the continent about two years, where his extravagance was so unbounded, that it became necessary to recall him ; and he had been married, one year, to the amiable lady before mentioned.

Mrs. Martindale was elated by Lord Darnley's attention to her. Her eyes sought him every where, and he perceived it ; nor was it long before an opportunity offered, that, in making him master of her person, banished the slender impression she had made on his mind. He met with little or no resistance when he hinted at a private assignation ; which being fixed, and effected at the house of her conve-

nient, milliner, paſſed without ſuſpicion a-
mong her attendants.

Lord Darnley was no ſooner a happy lover,
than he was a ſatiated one. He had never
ſeen any woman but Lady Darnley for whom
he had conceived a ſentiment beyond that of
momentary paſſion ; and had ſhe not been his
wife, it is moſt probable that in her alone, all
his inclinations would have centered ; but
how ſtrange is, it that every thing loſes a portion of its value from the moment we have an
indiſputeable claim on it ! The virtuous Lady
Darnley, who had not a particle of coquetry
in her diſpoſition, had married the man of her
choice, nor had ſhe a wiſh equal to that of
pleaſing him. We might be led to ſuppoſe
from the remark I have juſt made (and from
that only), that had he been more ſteady in
his conduct towards her, ſhe might have been
more indifferent. She knew that he had errors, but ſhe did not know the extent of them ;
and ſhe fondly hoped, that her unremiting attention to his happineſs, and conſtant properi-
ty of conduct, would at length overcome them:
She knew Lady Jane, and Mrs. Martindale,
by report only ; her approaching confinement,
which ſhe expected every hour, keeping her
conſtantly at home, without other ſociety
than her mother, who was come for the firſt
time in her life to London, for the purpoſe of
attending her at that trying moment.

When the newſpapers announced Lady
Darnley's delivery, Mrs. Martindale pleaſed

herfelf with the idea of monopolizing his lordfhip's conftant attendance ; and having mentioned to her hufband the polite attentions that
Lady Jane and herfelf had received from him,
fignified her intention of fending him a card for
the next evening fhe fhould receive company,
and of introducing his lordfhip to his acquaintance. To this no objection could be made, and
Mrs. Martindale took an early opportunity of
difpatching invitations to feveral of her acquaintance, among whom Lord Darnley was
not forgotten.

Lady Jane, who had no fufpicion of what
had paffed, and who really liked Lord Darnley, though fhe had not particularly appeared
to do fo, was glad of this opportunity of bringing Mr. James Martindale acquainted with him
alfo ; and of becoming by thefe means known
to Lady Darnley, when her confinement fhould
be over.

Mrs Martindale's affembly was brilliant in
the extreme ; for fhe had been very particular
on that occafion, and had herfelf felected from
her vifiting-book, fuch names as ftood foremoft
in the gaudy catalogue of rank.

At the appointed hour, fhe faw her rooms
fill to her heart's fatisfaction, but in vain fhe
looked for Lord Darnley !——She grew inat-
tentive to her vifitors, walked fuccefively
thro' the rooms, and looked continually at her
watch, which fhe fancied loft *time*. fhe could
not account for his abfence. It was on HIS ac-

count fhe had that evening affembled all that
was moft fafhionable in town, and had ftudied
to raife her confequence by the felection of her
company; yet he was the only perfon whodid
not appear. At eleven, the party began to
difperfe; the duchefs of G————and her lovely daughters were juft taking their leave, when
Lord Darnley was announced.

The fudden appearance of the fun breaking
through the thick clouds of a mifty morning,
could not convey a more genial warmth to the
dew-damp traveller, than did the fight of Lord
Darnley to Mrs. Martindale; her eyes bright-
ened as fhe led him towards Mr. Martindale,
who received him with the utmoft politenefs.
But the electrical fhock of mortification inftantly fucceeded, when, in a voice fcarcely arti-
culate, he enquired for Lady Jane. There
was an air of forrow and confufion in his countenance, that it was not poffible for her to mif-
conftrue. Mrs. Martindale had more pride
than love; and with a haughty fneer turning
haftily from him, fhe informed his lordfhip, that
fhe had laft feen Lady Jane at cards in the adjoining room. He immediately went there.
The party had juft broke up, and fhe was ftanding near the door (waiting for Mr. Martindale,
who was gone to enquire for the carriage),
when Lord Darnley approached her. He took
her hand, with a freedom fhe had never obferved in him, and in a faltering voice whifper-
ed—OH LADY JANE, IN YOU I HOPE TO
FIND A FRIEND!—Struck at his appearance,
which indicated a fenfibility of which fhe had

not hitherto fuppofed him capable, fhe eagerly afked, what could have thus affected him? The tears rufhed into his eyes, and he could only fay " Lady Darnley"—as Mr. Martindale informed her their carriage was up. She returned haftily to wifh Mrs. Martindale good-night; introduced Mr. James Martindale to Lord Darnley, who handed her into it, and they parted for the night.

C H A P. XV.

LORD Darnley did not return up ftairs, but defiring that his feryants might be called, threw himfelf into the carriage, and ordered it home. His heart was affected, and for once he facrificed the rules of politenefs to its feelings. When he arrived there, he flew to Lady Darnley's apartment, without having fpoken to any one ; but alas ! little did he expect the fcene that awaited him; He knocked gently at the door, fearful of difturbing her repofe : but receiving no anfwer, he opened it. The curtains were all undrawn. On one fide of the bed, he faw her mother grafping her hands ; on the other, the nurfe was chafing her temple with hartfhorn ;—but fhe, alas, was gone for ever !—A moment convinced him of the fatal truth ; the next that fucceeded it, deprived him of his fenfes.

It was on the ninth-day after Lady Darnley's delivery of her firſt child. Some unfavourable ſymptoms had appeared in the morning, but they were not ſuſiciently ſo to alarm the phyſicians, or nurſe, of any immediate danger. Yet a fatal preſentiment had taken poſſeſſion of Lord Darnley from the firſt hour ſince her lying-in; and this was ſtrengthened by ſome oblique, yet gentle hints that had been given him by the angle of purity herſelf; who had unfortunately ſtopped her cariage one morning by accident at the door of Mrs. Martindale's milliner, where ſhe bought ſome things, and gave a card, with orders that others ſhould be ſent to her. The oſficious Frenchwoman told her, that ſhe was ſure ſhe muſt be beholden to Lord Darnly, or Mrs. Martindale, for the honour of her ladyſhips cuſtom, as ſhe was that lady's milliner, and had frequently ſeen his lordſhip at her houſe.

I do not believe that this French milliner (or indeed any other milliner) could plead ignorance in ſuch a ſituation. She could not ſuppoſe that Lord Darnley (whoſe name had been mentioned to her by Mrs. Martindale) had met that lady there ſecretly, and in a private room, for any good purpoſe. No. But the diſcovery of the intrigue to Lady Darnley might prove in the end beneficial to her, and ſhe was not of a nature to reflect on the delicate feelings of *a woman of honour*. Theſe, were therefore to be ſacrificed to her own mercenary and barbarous diſpoſition; and ſhe planted a thorn in the breaſt of that ſpotleſs lady; it ſeſtered there, and was her companion to the grave.

Lady Darnley had a few days after the birth of her child, which was a daughter, moſt earneſtly implored her lord to promiſe her that he would never neglect this only pledge of their love. She conjured him to cheriſh her for her mother's ſake ; as ſhe had imbibed, ſhe ſaid a ſtrange idea, that her FIRST child would be alſo her LAST. She gently added (ſqueezing his hand, and convulſed almoſt with agony as ſhe ſpoke), that ſhe hoped he would in future point out to her a better example than the Mrs. Martindale whom ſhe had never ſeen, but of whom ſhe had heard MORE than ſhe thought proper to reveal to him, till after her recovery. Lord Darnley with truth declared, that he had never been in Mrs. Martindale's houſe ; that he had only formed a ſlight acquaintance with her at different public places ; but he did not mention the French milliner, nor any other circumſtance that could tend to corroborate their intimacy.

On the day that he received Mrs. Martindale's card, he was half inclined to ſhew it Lady Darnley ; but her weak health and ſpirits prevented him. Yet he had no juſt ground to ſuſpect her approaching diſſolution. Her phyſicians had not, as I ſaid, even hinted at danger; and if his mind was painfully awake to the apprehenſion of it, he could impute it only to thoſe fears which a timid ſuperſtition, and not reality, had induced him to give way to. He

F

told her that he was engaged to an affembly that evening, but he did not fay where; and his acquaintance was fo numerous, that without the help of the milliner, or fome of her confederates, Lady Darnley could not have fufpected it to be at Mrs. Martindale's fhe however DID fufpect it, and received private intelligence of that lady's houfe being open the fame evening, and that Lord Darnley's carriage made one of the number at her door.

When the meffenger who was fent to enquire into the truth of this unwelcome news returned from executing his commiffion, Lady Darnley infifted on feeing him; nor could the tender entreaties of her mother prevent her from diving into the truth. Her diforder (infeparable from her fituation) had that day taken a turn, and marked her death as certain; fhe received the information of it with all the fortitude that a mind already wafted to heaven could experience. She defired that Lord Darnley might be immediately fent for; and her footman, eager to obey the orders of his much-loved lady, haftened on the wings of anxiety to meet his lord. But when he reached Devonfhire Place, he heard only that he had been there for a very fhort time, and was returned. Lord Darnley was at home a few minutes before his fervant; but it was already too late for him to catch the expiring breath of his lovely, his virtuous, his already fainted wife!

His grief became unbounded; he kiffed her pale lips, and invoked the God of Heaven to

witnefs the integrity of his heart !—He had
been guilty of errors, he felt he had, of fatal
ones ; but little did he imagine what would be
their dreadful confequences; for, in the firft
paroxfyms of phrenfy, he condemned himfelf
as being the fole author of her death. He ordered his little girl to be brought into the room,
and kiffed her with an enthufiaftic and fervent
affection. He joined her little face to that of
her fenfelefs mother; and pointed out each
refembling feature. It was a folemn, an awful fcene ; and he was at length forced out of
the room ; his expreffions of grief becoming fo
violent, as to threaten with injury his own
health.

Lord Darnley would not be told, nor fuffer
himfelf to refleƈt, that an over delicate confti-
tution had foon furrendered itfelf to a malady,
which was fo powerful as to bafile every effort
of art. To this was to be imputed Lady Darnley's early death. His feeling heart taught
him firft to confider his own mifconduƈt ; and
he alternately upbraided his child, and himfelf,
as the authors of their irreparable lofs.

MR S. Martindale feldom or ever took up a newfpaper; and a cold (of which fhe made the moft) had confined her for fome days at home; during which fhe did not fee Lady Jane, who was gone to pafs a week at Oxford, on a vifit to one of Mr. Martindale's brother collegians.

On the evening of their return, they went to Devonfhire Place, and ftaid fupper. Mrs. Martindale appointed two o'clock the next day to call on Lady Jane, as they were to go together to befpeak dreffes for the enfuing mafquerade.

When Mrs. Martindale arrived in Argyle Street, fhe found Lady Jane in tears; who told her that Mr. Martindale was juftgone out to enquire into the truth of a paragraph they had obferved in *The World*, which mentioned Lady Darnley's death. They did not however wait his return, but ftepped into the carriage as foon as it arrived, ordering the coachman to drive flowly towards Cavendifh Square; and to ftop, if he faw his mafter. At the entrance of it, they were met by a hearfe, adorned with white plumes and efcutcheons,

and followed by many coaches and weeping attendants. The footman's enquiries were anfwered by the name of *Lady Darnley.*

Lady Jane let down the fore-glafs, and ordered the coachman to return; but Mrs. Martindale defired that he might firft proceed to
Donnelly's in Taviftock Street; having no
idea, fhe faid, of being difappointed of her mafquerade drefs, becaufe Lady Darnley (a woman whom fhe had never feen) was dead.
Lady Jane endeavoured as much as pofllible to
conceal her grief; fearing to exprefs even a
fentiment of pity, left it fhould be conftrued into one of love, for a man for whom fhe had
hitherto felt nothing more than a fifterly affection : but whofe prefent misfortune was in itfelf fufficient to intereft a heart poffeffed of lefs
exquifite feelings than her own.

Mrs. Martindale ordered a Turkifh habit.
Lady Jane did not order any thing. She fhould
be contented, fhe faid, to appear as an humble
attendant on the fair Grecian, not having at
that time fpirits to encounter the wit of the
different characters fhe fhould meet with
there..

They returned to Argyle Street, and parted
at the door. Mr. Martindale was at home,
expecting Lady Jane. He perceived her melancholy, and enquired its caufe. She candidly told him, that Lady Darnley's fudden
death, and the funeral which fhe had met, had
uncommonly affected her. She was engaged,
fhe faid, to a party going that evening to the

Dùchefs of G———'s, but fhe found herfelf
unequal to it; and was going to fend a card of
apology. This fhe did, and they paſſed the
remainder of the day in a domeſtic, but not a
very cheerful tête-à-tête. -

The next morning, while Mr. Martindale
was out, a fervant of Lord Darnley brought a
note from him to Lady Jane, requeſting that
he might be permitted to wait on her for a few
minutes, if fhe was alone and difengaged. His
ſituation-precluded the poſſibility of a denial,
had fhe not even wifhed to fee him. There is
an undefcribable pleafure attendant only on
minds fufceptible of fine feelings, in liftening
to a tale of woe, and fympathizing with the
pathetic narrator. Lord Darnley, the happy
and the acknowledged admirer of Mrs. Martindale, had not excited in Lady Jane any
alarming fenfation ; but Lord Darnley mifera-
ble, and felecting HER as a friend in his misfortunes, might become a dangerous companion.

In lefs than half an hour, Lord Darnley was
in Argyle Street. Lady Jane gave orders that
no perfon fhould be admitted, and was almoſt
equally affected with himfelf. He took this
opportunity to unbofom himfelf to her. He
faid, that whatever might be the fentiments of
his heart towards her, he confidered that in
his prefent ſituation, and her own, an avowal
of them would be a violation of decency both
to themfelves and to the memory of the dear
departed, who was then only on the road to

her quiet home !—But the intercourfe of friendfhip was not to be prohibited, and he felt THAT
of Lady Jane was neceffary for the prefervation of his exiftance ; which he valued only for
the fake of the haplefs infant that had furvived
its mother. He then lamented in the moft affecting manner the fatal error of a moment,
that had tempted him to beftow a thought on
the DISSIPATED, the UNPRINCIPLED *Mrs.
Martindale* !—(Here Lady Jane gazed on him
with aftonifhment.)—He hoped, he faid, that
her generous heart would inftruct her to pardon
a connection into which he had been inadvertently drawn, at the fame time that (he could
not help owning it) fhe alone was the object of
his refpect and admiration ; and that it would
teach her to feel for a man who had NOW a
claim on her pity, but who had hitherto deferved her utmoft contempt. He then told her
of the converfation he had held with Lady
Darnley, foon after her lying-in, and among
the number of his confeffions, the French milliner was not forgotten.

Lady Jane was too much confufed by what
fhe had heard, to know in what manner to reply to him. She had too high an opinion of
his *honour* to doubt his *word* ; yet fhe could not
have fuppofed that Mrs. Martindale would have
carried her imprudence beyond what fhe had
conceived to be an unmeaning levity. Yet
how neceffary did it appear to her at this moment for an entire explanation to take place,
when Lord Darnley implored her pardon for
having dared to furmife that fhe had been the

confidante of that vile woman ; who had not
fcrupled to declare to him, that Lady Jane had
admited more than one favoured lover ; but
that her regard and'pity for both Mr. Martindales had prevented her hitherto divulging
what in the courfe of time could not fail to be
publicly known.

Lady Jane could not without the moft poig-
nant emotion here that her fair fame had been
traduced ; and by the woman too who fhould
have been the firft to defend it. How cruel,
how defperate was her condition ! for, while
Lord Darnley was fpeaking, fhe recollected
having obferved that feveral of her female acquaintance had latterly behaved towards her
with uncommon referve. although no one had
been friendly enough to intimate in what fhe
had offended. But fhe had not fuffered it at
the time to make any great impreffion on her ;
as fhe was perfectly confcious of her innocence,
and attributed it only to fome trivial caufe,
with which fhe might poffibly hereafter become acquainted.

But now fhe felt mortified indeed ! She
found that Lord Darnley had been the FIRST
perfon prejudiced againft her, and fhe could
have wifhed it to be the reverfe. In HIS eyes,
fhe wanted to appear perfect. She knew not
how to exculpate herfelf from calumnies fo at-
rocious, nor how to convince Lord Darnley of
the falfehood of her accufer. She entreated
his lordfhip to make allowances for the agitati-
on into which his difcourfe had thrown her, as

an apology for the little she could at that moment urge in her juftification; she requefted his advice how to act, and inwardly refolved, let what would be the confequence, to abide by it. She begged he would direct her how to proceed in a matter of fuch importance to the peace of the whole family ; obferving that she was too inexperienced to judge for herfelf; and that in confequence of the avowal he had made, she conceived him to be the only perfon who was able (or who indeed might be willing) to advife her.

He told her, that he faw no alternative between a feparation taking place among them all, or her eternal filence on the fubject. He begged for God's fake that she would not expofe herfelf to farther infults and mortifications ; but that she would fuffer herfelf to be wholly advifed by him, and continue to live as before: at the fame time he exacted a promife from her, that she would immediately acquaint him by letter, should any new manœuvres of Mrs. Martindale's intervene, to render the difcovery of her treachery unavoidable.

Lady Jane promifed faithfully to adhere to all he faid, he then entreated her to honour his little girl fometimes with her attention. He was going he faid to let his houfe in Cavendifh Square, and to fend her with her nurfe to that of a gardener at Liffon-Green, near Paddington, in whofe wife he could confide. She was to remain there fome time, as he was going out of town the next day, to pafs a few months at the head quarters of his regiment. He then a- rofe to take his leave of Lady Jane ; gave her the child's direction ; and refpectfully, but pre- cipitately withdrew.

Lady Jane was no fooner alone, than fhe gave vent to her opprefled heart. But Lord Darnley had enjoined on her the hardeft tafk poffible to a generous mind, that of diffimulati- on, and fhe faw herfelf for the firft time obliged to practife it. She was compelled therefore to command her feelings, and to endeavour to compofe her appearance. Her heart was to become the fole repofitory of thofe cares, which, alas ! fhe had not a friend to divide.

When Mr. Martindale returned home, he ironically afked Lady Jane, whom fhe had feen ?—She mentioned Lord Darnley's vifit, but in her confufion omitted telling him of his requeft that fhe fhould fometimes fee his child. He obferved that her eyes were red with weep- ing ; but how, he faid, could it be otherwife, while fhe made Lord Darnley's griefs her own ? She began to excufe herfelf ; he fcarcely deigned to anfwer her, and withdrew to his apartment.

Several weeks paffed without any change taking place. Lady Jane often pondered on the extraordinary confeffion that had been made her ; but fhe ftrictly fulfilled her promife, and buried her fecret within her aching breaft. She even endeavoured as far as it was poffible to banifh the remembrance of it. She never

,even hinted to Mrs. Martindale, that she suf-pected her misconduct ; and judging from the purity of her own heart, she wished, rather than she hoped, that it might be the last failing of which she should be ever able to accuse her. She was even so generous in her sentiments as in THAT ERROR of Mrs. Martindale's to find an excuse for her cruelty towards herself. She knew that it was impossible for so young and so beautiful a woman to be fond of a husband who was old enough to be her grandfather ; and she was convinced that it proceeded solely from a jealousy that had arisen in consequence of the love she bore Lord Darnley. The more she reflected on HIS advanatges, the less she won-dered at the choice Mrs. Martindale had made.

C H A P. XVII.

MR. Martindale became overbearing, and was at times even infolent to Lady Jane. She was no longer in HIS opinion the amiable *Contraſt* to Mrs. Martindale ; he conceived her virtues to diminiſh, and her beauties to decay. Yet he was the only one who fuſpected either, or who had at leaſt [dared to fay ſo. I ſhould indeed except Mrs. Martindale ; who not only viewed her with the eye of hatred, but who alſo became indefatigable in her endeavours to poiſon the mind both of the old gentleman and his ſon againſt her. Yet ſhe took her meaſures ſo artfully, that Lady Jane had no reaſon to ſuppofe ſhe ever held any private converſation with them about her.

They were one evening at the Ducheſs of G———'s, and Lady Jane was particularly ſtruck with the appearance of a young lady, who never ceaſed to look at her. She enquired her name, and found that it was *Miſs Stuart*. She requeſted another lady to introduce them to each other, and particularly aſked after the Colonel. She would have added another name to his, but her refolution forſook her. A far- ther acquaintance was mutually propoſed, and accepted, and Mr. Martindale waited on Colonel Stuart, at his lodgings in Cumberland-ftreet, the next day. But he did not condefcended to inform Lady Jane at his return of what had paffed there, neither did he once mention the name of *Glencairn*.

In a few days Lady Jane paid a morning vifit to Mifs Stuart, having left a card there the preceding evening. She was admitted, and found that lovely girl fitting at a frame for embroidery. Glencairn was reading to her, and the Colonel was examining different charts which lay on the table. Lady Jane coloured. Glencairn was vifibly agitated, and inftantly turning to the Colonel, folicited him to walk out; to which the other affenting, they foon difappeared.

Mifs Stuart, with the freedom of youth and innocence, gave Lady Jane a long account of her travels, which were, fhe faid, pathetically ended by her witneffing the folemn fcene of her friend Mifs Beaumont's renunciation of this life, to purfue, according to her own ideas, the fureft road to happinefs in the next.

They were talking over this, and other matters, when the poftman's knock announced letters; and a fervant delivered one to Mifs Stuart, which Lady Jane entreated her to read without ceremony. She faid it was from Mifs Beaumont (whofe name was changed to mother Saint Etienne), congratulating herfelf and family on their fafe return to England, and lamenting the probability that exifted of

G

her feeing them no more. She read it throughout; and then gave it to Lady Jane, requefting her to perufe that charming fpecimen of female friendfhip and letter-writing. In it, the
following paffage fixed all her attention:

    " The only point, my dear Mifs Stuart,
" on which we could ever difagree during our
" long refidence together in this peaceful con-
" vent, was that of my feclufion from the
" world. When I declared to you that my
" refolution was fixed on taking the veil, how
" many dangerous objections did you not hold
" out to me, in hopes to alter the fettled pur-
" pofe of my heart! You invited me to live
" with you, and moft tenderly affured me,
" that no future change in your fituation
" fhould be able to effect one in your fentiments
" towards me. Nor was this the only allure-
" ment you placed before me. Alas! you em-
" ployed a more dangerous one ftill, by en-
" deavouring to unite the duties of religion
" and worldly affection. You went fo far as
" to affure me, that my facrifice would be ac-
" ceptable to God himfelf; who, you fay,
" fent us into this world for the benefit of fo-
" ciety; fo that we have no more right to ab-
" ftract ourfelves from it, than we have to lay
" down our life when we are weary of it.
" The world, you told me, abounds with
" pure and focial delights; but they can be on-
" ly enjoyed by thofe who hold an intercourfe
" with it. Yet have you not fometimes, my
" dear friend, inadvertently owned to me that
" you are not happy?—And if you, formed

" by nature for all its bleffings, are not fo,
" how can you imagine that I, a ftranger even
" in idea, fhould be willing to renounce for it
" a way of life that I have been taught to be-
" lieve is preferable to every other? You
" went fo far as to affure me, that your heart
" has made its choice, and unfortunately fixed
" itfelf where it has no hope of return. That
" the only man to whom you could wifh to
" unite yourfelf is, as you have every reafon
" to believe, attached elfewhere; and that
" you fufpect, from the hints he has given,
" that the object of his love is— *married!*

" Would not this idea, my dear Mifs Stuart,
" rather frighten a young novice from the
" world, than encourage her to enter it?—I
" have read of love, though I never felt its in-
" fluence; and I am thankful that I have nei-
" ther the inclination nor the power to add
" one to its nnmberlefs victims."

Lady Jane perufed this part of the letter
with particular emotion; fhe too furely gueffed
that it alluded to Glencairn and herfelf, of
which fhe was fully convinced when Mifs Stuart afked her *What fhe thought of Glencairn?*
This queftion, which might not have paffed for
fingular, had it not been accompanied with an
uneafy air of conftraint that denoted an over
anxious curiofity, fuffufed Lady Jane's countenance with confcious blufhes, that did not
efcape the penetrating eyes of Mifs Stuart.
Each had fpoken fufficiently plain to be under-
ftood by the other, that neither was fatisfied.

G 2

Lady Jane's filence. and vifible embarraffment were as expreffive as could be the moft eloquent language. The letter had thrown them into a ftate of uneafy perplexity; it had difturbed their peace, and was from that moment the fubject to both of many paintul reflections.

Lady Jane frequently met Glencairn; and fhe could not perceive without emotion, and forrow, the tender langour that clouded his fine countenance; confidering as fhe did, that his attachment to her was the fole caufe of it. Her heart feemed divided between him and Lord Darnley. She was unconfcious of giving the preference to either, and fhe indulged the pure fentiments of innocent affection for both. Mrs. Martindale was continually fabricating tales to her difadvantage; fhe reprefented Lord Darnley to her acquaintance as an unprincipled libertine, who had taken an advantage of the introduction fhe had given him in her houfe, and had endeavoured by hints too plain to be mifconftrued, to feduce her affections from it. She fincerely wifhed, fhe faid, that Lady Jane might not be deceived in the more favourable opinion fhe had formed of him; for fhe intimated that her ladyfhip entertained a very high one. Mrs. Martindale did not openly inveigh againft her, for that might have led to a conviction of the truth; but fhe wounded her under the mafk of apparent regard; and while fhe flattered and careffed her, fhe murdered her repofe, and meditated her final deftruction.

T H E S E ladies continued to be as much together as formerly, and time appeared to have almost obliterated the remembrance; of Lord Darnley, when a circumstance interfered-that was laudable in its cause, but most pernicious in its effect. Lady Jane had as I before obd served) neglected mentioning to her husband the promise she had made him, of sometimes visiting his daughter. Her time had indeed been so much taken up with other engagements, that she had not yet found a leisure hour to attend to it. She however one morning felt a strong inclination to fee the child ; ordered the carriage, and went to Paddington. She found the little cherub looking perfectly well, and staid with it above an hour. She then defired the nurse would make Mifs Darnley, and herfelf, ready to accompany her ; that she would take them for an airing a little farther on the road, and fet them down on her return.

They had not proceeded half a mile, before they were met by Mrs. Martindale's carriage, who was in it, with her old man. They both stopped ; and Mrs. Martindale, giving a significant look at her husband, observed, *How extreamly odd it was, that they should meet by accident on the same road.* Her eyes were in-

ftantly directed to the nurfe and child ; and
both of them appearing in deep mourning, did
not leave a doubt who they were. She propofed their returning in Lady Jane's coach, and
fending back their own ; which was complied
with. Her motive for doing this, was to dif-
cover where the child lived. But in that fhe
was difappointed ; Lady Jane having determined at that moment to take it to Argyle-ftreet.
She therefore ordered the coachman to drive
there, telling the nurfe fhe would fend them
fafe back in the evening.

As foon as fhe returned home, fhe fent the
nurfe into the Steward's room, and, taking
the child in her arms, went into Mr. Martindale's drefling-room, and begged leave to introduce a ftranger to his acquaintance, the
infant daughter of Lord Darnley. She faid
this with a vifible confufion, which arofe in
confequence of feeling herfelf obliged to. relate
the circumftance of meeting Mr. and Mrs.
Martindale, without which it was poffible for
him to furmife that he would not have been
informed of her vifit. He took but little notice of the fmileing girl, who was in the evening reconducted with her nurfe, to the place
of their deftination.

C H A P. XIX.

THE gentle Mifs Stuart became every day more attached to Glencairn, while Mr. Courtenay, an intimate acquaintance of her father's was as paffionately in love with her: Mr. Courtenay was a gentleman of Ireland, of confiderable fortune, but defcended from an obfcure family, and many years older than Mifs. Stuart. Yet fuch was the nature of Mary, that thefe difadvantages, had even the want of money been annexed to them, would have been no impediment to her union with him, had her father wifhed it, and her affections been difengaged. But fhe cherifhed the flatterer, Hope. She believed all that it fuggefted, and fhe really thought that fhe fhould yet fee the day, when Glencairn would renounce his attachment, of which fhe was no longer uncertain as to the object. Alas! the rofes began once more to fade on her lavely cheek; her fpirits gradually forfook her; and her father, perceiving both, at length tenderly queftioned her. He mentioned Glencairn, and entreated to be informed of the fituation of her mind, refpecting him.

Mifs Stuart's heart repofed on the bofom of this indulgent father; fhe acknowledged to him

her attachment for Glencairn ; but fhe affured
him, that fhe poffeffed too much pride ever to
fuffer that attachment to overcome her reafon.
She had obferved an indifference in his manner
towards her, that had confiderably augmented
fince their return to England ; and fhe was determined rather to facrifice her peace for ever,
than to confent, were he even to urge it, to
owe the happinefs of being his, to a fentiment
of pity oniy, with which fhe might infpire
him.   Glencairn's heart was, fhe was well
affured, devoted to another.   She did not wifh
to difavow that *he* alone would ever remain the
object of her moft fervent affections ; but fhe
would never owe the gratification of indulging
them to the chance that deprived him of poffeffing that more fortunate woman, and to a
fentiment that muft render her acceptance of
him defpicable in her own eyes, and ftill more
fo in her father's.

Sentiments fuch as thefe could not fail to
ftrengthen in Colonel Stuart, that opinion of
his lovely daughter, which had hitherto fallen
little fhort of adoration.   He coincided in all fhe
faid, and gloried in the accomplifhment of his
wifhes.   For what wifh could be fo dear to him,
as that of feeing his Mary, though ftruggling
with ftrong paffions, heroic enough to fubdue
them ?   He preffed her to his bofom, ond affured her, that he preferred her happinefs to every worldly confideration ; but that there was
one beyond the limits of this life, which hung
heavy on his mind.   He alluded to the period
of his own exiftance, which from the courfe of

nature, and his own habitual complaints, was not likely to be prolonged many years. To fee his Mary fettled, was to enfure a happy termination of his days; to leave her without a protector, would embitter his laft moments, the approach of which he wifhed to meet without a pang, as they haftened him to a re-union with her angelic mother!

As he uttered the laft fentence, the tears quivered in his expreffive eyes, and gently forced their paffage down his venerable cheeks. Mary felt the weight of his argument, but could not command refolution enough to fay fhe would accept the thrice-proffered hand of Mr. Courtenay: fhe conjured the Colonel never to mention the fubject of their converfation to any one; and fhe ftill hoped, fhe faid, that fhe might be at length enabled to eradicate from her mind thofe ideas which fhe had hitherto fo rafhly and fo fondly entertained. But fhe did not tell him ALL fhe thought; her heart had made its election, and fhe knew that every endeavour would be vain to contend againft it. She inwardly determined to cherifh the remembrance of Glencairn, and, leaving the chance of their future union to himfelf, fhe in fecret refolved never to enter into an engagement that might on her fide impede it.

It was impoffible for Glencairn to be ignorant of the attachment he had infpired, neither did he attempt to appear fo. He deeply lamented it, and, with a candcur feldom practifed among elegant young men, he affured Colonel Stuart that his friendſhip for the lovely Mary exceeded even the bounds of brotherly love. He wiſhed, he ſaid, for the ſake of his own peace, and he believed he might without vanity include that of Mary alſo, that his heart had not been entangled in a fatal attachment, from whence he was never likely to derive a hope of happineſs ; he added, that he had too delicate a ſenſe of honour to offer her his hand, while he had not a heart to beſtow with it. Miſs Stuart, he juſtly obſerved, merited the firſt offerings of the pureſt. How could he propoſe to make her wretched, by endeavouring to unite her to a man who had it not in his power to forget another ; and for whom his love was ſo criminal, that at the ſame time he owned it to his friend, he felt a degree of remorſe at leaſt equal to it ?

Colonel Stuart ſincerely pitied, and endeavoured to ſooth him, for he too had once felt the force of an irreſiſtible attachment. He propoſed their immediately returning to Scotland, where time, diſtance from the beloved objeĉt, and the growing affeĉtions of Mary, might poſſibly lead him to a recovery of his reaſon. Alas," replied Glencairn, " how can " I expeĉt the countenance of your too gene-" rous regard ? Were I to return with you to " that ſeat of innocence and virtue, ſhould I " not inſult the feelings of your angelic daugh-" ter ? Sould I not carry with me there the " wound that *Lady Jane Martindale* has made " in my peace?—Yes, my dear Sir, you are " entitled to my confidence, and you ſhall

" wholly poffefs it. It was *fhe* who firft infpi-
" red me with love ; to *her* I am determined
" to devote my exiftence ; and for her fake a-
" lone, I will forego the happinefs that flatter-
" ing fortune has placed within my view. I
" will bid an everlafting adieu to the all-
" fafcinating Mary : I will pray to Heaven
" that fhe may fix her choice on a more fortu-
" nate man ; and that fhe may forget, yes,
" for ever forget, the one who now reliquifh-
" es, becaufe he feels himfelf unworthy of
" her."

Colonel Stuart liftened with aftonifhment to
the confeffion he had heard ; and when he
reflected that Glencairn's fole dependance was
on himfelf, his heart was filled with the fond-
eft efteem for his character. Souls, he faid,
fuch as thofe of Glencairn and his daughter,
were furely paired in heaven. Earthly viciffi-
tudes might for a time feperate,-but never
could wholly difunite them ; and his mind,
fanguine as Mary's, ftill prefaged a certainty of
future felicity. But, from Glencairn, nothing could be at prefent expected. When Colonel Stuart faw that he was bent in following
his fate, he infifted, in token of their mutual
friendfhip, as well as of the tender regard he
bore to the memory of his deceafed father, that
he fhould accept from him a fmall annuity of
one hundred pounds ; and he extorted from
him a promife, that fhould he perceive any alteration in his fentiments refpecting Lady Jane
Martindale, that he would return to him as
his fon. To fpare the delicacy of Mary, it was

neceffary to invent fome planfible ftory ; and they agreed to inform her, that unforefeen bu- finefs relative to a friend in Scotland (whom they named) would detain Glencairn longer in London, than it would be convenient for the Colonel to ftay there. She received the intel- ligence with lefs furprife than they expected, and her father fignified to her his intention o returning to Allanbank the week follow- ing.

'On the evening before they were to fet out, they all appeared alike affected at their approch- ing feparation. Glencairn knew too well his influence over the heart of Mary, not to dread that her feelings would be overpowered by it ; and he mentioned as by chance to the Colonel, before her, that he hoped to join them in Scot- land within a month. While he fpoke, he caft a fide-look at Mifs Stuart ; he faw her colour change, and the tears which fhe vainly endea- voured to fupprefs. run down her cheeks. He haftily called for a candle ; pretended a drowfinefs he was never farther from feeling, and rofe to take his leave. He kiffed Mifs Stuart with the moft fervent affection ; preffed the Colonel's hand to his heart ; and a tear fell on it : he foftly articulated the word *fare- well*—and retired to his bed-chamber, where he threw himfelf on the fofa, and indulged the *effufions of a heart torn by anguifh and defpaire.*

C H A P XX.

GLENCAIRN remained near an hour in this ftate of agonizing reflection, and was at length roufed from it by hearing Colonel Stuart and his daughter retire to their apartments. He had been reflecting ferioully on his prefent fituation, and on every thing that had paffed ; but above all, on the fatherly tendernefs he had ever experienced from Colonel Stuart, and the recent proof of it ; on the fincere affection of his lovely daughter ;—on the fituation of Lady Jane Martindale—*a married woman !*—on the diffipated courfe of life fhe led ;—the cold indifference with which fhe appeared to receive his laft vifit ;—and the hints that had been given him, which gained ground every day, and appeared to taint the purity of her character. All thefe confiderations darted like a ray of light on his bewildered mind, and he formed the RESOLUTION to throw himfelf at the fame moment at Colonel Stuart's feet, and to implore from him the hand of his daughter. It was a fudden and a violent decifion, that admitted not of reflection. He dreaded to meet with oppofition from his heart, fhould he confult it ; he was no ftranger to its weeknefs, and he felt that it required all his fortitude to enable him to accomplifh his prefent purpofe.

Fired by the momentary impulfe, he went to the door of Colonel Stuart's apartment, and gently knocking there, requefted admiflion, and attention to what he had to communicate.

The Colonel was not in bed; he had juft rifen from his knees, where it was his nightly cuftom to proftrate himfelf before his God, in fervent meditation. He was fomewhat furprifed at feeing Glencairn, who had not yet begun to undrefs, and who, apologizing for his intrufion, proceeded to fupplicate that he might find in him the tender advocate, not the inflexible judge.

He then told him that the purport of his nocturnal vifit was to implore once more his farther protection and advice. He begged that he would affift him to follow his own example, and point out to him the path of rectitude which fhould direct him to fhun the dangerous practices of a world he had already reafon to fuppofe a deceitful one. He affured him, that he had ferioufly pondered on the fentiments of his heart, and was convinced that on the exertions of his reafon his future happinefs depended. He was now determined to purfue that line of conduct that would be moft pleafing to his friend and benefactor, and was come to intreat his permiflion to return with him to Scotland; where he doubted not but reafon would foon teach him to overcome a mad attachment, of which he had feen the folly, and was therefore refolved to fubdue.

Colonel Stuart learned with rapture this happy affurance of his pupil's return to virtue; and
fo indulgent was this excellent man to thofe
failings he had never known, that he would
have confidered himfelf the author of his deftruction, had he not, accepted his proffered re-
pentance. How many virtuous minds are de-
ftroyed by the want of this indulgence! and
how much more laudable is it in a parent, or a
friend, to draw a veil over the faults of youth,
than to expofe them in the face of day, and,
inftead of diminifhing, augment them by their
unkindnefs! What a contraft to thofe characters in fuch a man as Colonel Stuart! He
might be juftly defcribed as poffeffing a thoufand virtues, without a fingle fault; or, if he
HAD a fault, it proceeded from the unbounded
benevolence of his heart, which taught him to
view mankind in general with an eye of affection, of which few were deferving. But though
he had experienced like others the poifonous
effects of ingratitude, he had not yet learned to
think ill even of thofe who had proved themfelves unworthy of having known him. His
houfe, his heart, and his purfe, were alike extended to all; and it was fortunate for himfelf,
and his family, that he was a ftranger in the
gay world, where he muft have inevitably fallen a prey to the defigning. His way of life
was fuited to his fituation and circumftances,
and that life was fpent in doing good.

It is no wonder, then, that Glencairn, who
poffeff'd his moft tender regard fhould not meet
with any difficulty in perfuading him of the
ftability of his inclinations. They parted for

the night under the moft comfortable fenfations; the one, fatisfied that he had acted up to
his duty; the other, that he had faved a generous mind from perdition. Colonel Stuart
fancied that he had fnatched Glencairn from
the edge of a precipice; and Glencairn fancied
that he had fubdued every blameable pro-
penfity—Alas, poor human nature!

WHEN Mifs Stuart rofe in the morning, fhe was furprized that Glencairn was to accompany them. Her heart rejoiced, as fhe interpreted this change in his intentions to the impoffibility he found of leaving her. Their journey was a pleafant one ; it was wholly undifturbed by care or regret, for fhe had left nothing in London that could tempt her to wifh ever to return there. But her fenffibility was painfully tried, when fhe firft beheld Allanbank. The old houfe-keeper, who had lived there ever fince the Colonel's marriage, welcomed her home with unfeigned joy. She conducted her towards the apartment that had been formerly her late miftrefs's ; but when they approached the door of it, Mifs Stuart gave a faint fhriek, and fainted in her arms. The worthy Mrs. M'Kenzie was alarmed, but would not open the ill-clofed wounds of her venerable mafter's heart, by making him witnefs a fcene that fhe knew would be only momentary. She returned to the room where fhe had left the gentlemen, and giving an expreffive look at Glencairn, he inftantly followed her. She conducted him up ftairs, where they found Mifs Stuart attended by a houfe-maid, and beginning to recover. Glencairn flew to

H 3

support her with the tenderest care. She rais-
ed her fine eyes, first to Heaven, as if to invoke
the sainted spirit of her mother, and then turned them with ineffable sweetness upon him ; he
felt all that she would exprefs, and his feelings
were worked up to the highest pitch of grate-
ful enthusiasm. He involuntarily dropped on
one knee before her, and taking her hand in
his, he supplicated the Almighty to strengthen
him in his refolution, that he would never, never forsake her ! He arose when he had uttered this prayer. It came from the inmost re-
cesses of his heart, and had been pronounced
in too awful a manner for him to retract it ;
neither would he have done fo at that moment,
for the poffeffion of Lady Jane Martindale herself. Mifs Stuart had heard the blessed found ;
it sunk from her ear to her heart ; she received,
and cherifhed it there, as an old friend whom
she had been long expecting, and who was at
length returned to forsake her no more.

She was now enabled to look over her apartment with more compofure. Her piano-forte
had been placed there by the Colonel's order,
that she might be reconciled to the fight of it.
Glencairn went to his flute, and they passed an
hour in that happy harmony proceeding from
the union of fouls. When alone, Glencairn
took the opportunity of offering his heart and
hand to Mary. With what modest joy did she
accept the tender affurances of both ! She longed to rufh into her father's arms, and tell him
of her promifed felicity ; but virgin delicacy
laid a reftraint on her inclinations, and she left

to Glencairn the bleſſed taſk of making him happy ; for ſhe well knew that his heart, like her own, had been long ſet on their union. He was not leſs anxious than herſelf to impart their converſation to the Colonel, which he did not however find an opportunity of doing, till after Miſs Stuart had left them for the night.

Colonel Stuart received the declaration with an air of reſerve that ſurprized Glencairn, and filled him with confuſion. He deſired that he would allow himſelf time to reflect ſeriouſly on the nature of the ſolemn engagement into which he ſo ſuddenly and ſo lightly appeared to wiſh to enter. He conſidered it, he ſaid, a duty incumbent on him to admoniſh them both, and to exhort them to do nothing raſhly ; and how could he avoid believing that Glencairn only deceived himſelf in his preſent ideas, when little more than a week had elapſed ſincehe had in the moſt ingenuous manner acknowledged his inviolable attachment to Lady Jane Martindale ? How was he to reconcile ſuch inconſiſtencies ?—He added, that he had too high an opinion of the mind he had taken pride and pleaſure to adorn, to imagine for a moment that ſelf-intreſt would have the power to bias one of his actions ; at the ſame time he owned that his daughter was in that point worthy his attention ; and if he doubted his love for her, it proceeded from a fear that he did not know himſelf ſufficiently to be able to anſwer for his future conduct towards her throughout life.

Glencairn endeavoured to wave theſe ſeeming objections. He could not, he faid, difavow his firft inclination, but he had (at leaft he thought he had) fubdued it. They parted with a promife from the Colonel, that in the conver-fation he fhould have with Mifs Stuart on the fubject, he would not fay any thing that might tend to impede their mutual happinefs. In-deed the Colonel knew enough of his daughter's fentiments to be convinced, that although no-thing could alter her love for Glencairn, were he once to exert his parental authority, and forbid her to marry him, fhe would obey him, though at the certain expenfe of her happinefs, and the probable one of her life.

Colonel Stuart, the next morning, when breakfaft was over, requefted his daughter's at-tendance in his ftudy, where they remained a confiderable time, during which Glencairn did not find his fituation of fufpenfe perfectly com-fortable. He was at length relieved from it by their appearance, and he perceived that they had both been in tears. The Colonel took a hand of each of his children (as he was wont to call them), and joining them, he with humid eyes beftowed on each his bleffing. He could not fay much, for his heart was full, but he defired that their marriage might take place in two months from that time ; fome neceffary ar-rangement with refpect to his fortune being in-difpenfable previous to that event. Glencairn faluted the blufhing Mary ; they mutually embraced, and thanked the Colonel, and the day was fpent as may be fuppofed from thefe virtuous minds, each deriving comfort from the happinefs of the other.

Nothing appeared to be wanting at Allenbank to complete the extent of human felicity. Miſs Stuart became more intereſting as ſhe was more beloved ; for though Glencairn was conſcious that he ſhould not lead her to the altar with that enthuſiaſtic paſſion that borders on madneſs, and which ſeldom laſts long, his eſteem for, and his opinion of her augmented daily ; and Colonel Stuart's winter of life which had been hurried on by grief more than age, appeared on this occaſion to be impeded in its progreſs by a renovating ſpring. They had few viſitors at Allanbank ; ſome poor Scotch lairds were their principle neighbours, who having never gone beyond the Highlands, were ſo ignorant and uninformed, that their ſociety was rather courted through benevolence, than diſclaimed through pride. It was the intention of the family to paſs ſome of the next winter months at Edinburgh. The Colonel had a numerous acquaintance there in Mrs. Stuart's lifetime ; but ſince he had loſt her, and was ſeparated from his daughter, he neglected every worldly concern. They would not, however, find it difficult to meet with ſociety, whenever they viſited that charming city ; for their virtues ſecured them friends, wherever they appeared.

I HAVE already obferved, that the conduct of Mr. Martindale towards Lady Jane was wholly altered. A vifible coolnefs had taken place, and her ears were perpetually affailed by the enumeration of Mrs Martindale's virtues. Whatever fhe faid, was a law both to her hufband and his fon, and Lady Jane's life became more infupportable, as her fenfibility acquired more ftrength. She had latterly contracted an intimacy with the two Mifs Fieldings, daughters to the late Admiral of that name. They had been intimates of Lady Darnley. The eldeft was remarkably accomplifhed; fhe was almoft unrivalled on the harpficord, and feemed to poffefs a foul capable of the moft refined fentiments. Lady Jane was very partial to this young lady, who appeared to be greatly affected by her fituation. She frequently mentioned her diflike to Mrs. Martindale; and though Lady Jane had ftrictly avoided even hinting at her mifconduct with Lord Darnley, Mifs Fielding gave her reafon to fuppofe that fhe was not ignorant of it.

It was now Lent; and Mifs Fielding was very conftant in her attendance at the Oratorios.

She had one evening folicited Lady Jane's company in her box at Dury-Lane, who had latterly feldom gone into public, but was tempted
to accept the invitation, as Giornovich, whom
fhe had never feen, was to play there. She
had heard much of that charming performer,
but found that report, fo lavifh in his praife,
was yet unequal to convey a juft idea of his me-
rit. It was *The Meffiah* that was performed;
and at the end of the third part of it, that di-
vine mufician, with an enchanting harmony
that can be equalled only in heaven, varied the
plaintive *lullaby* in a manner fo exquifitely pathetic, as to draw tears from the feeling heart
of Lady Jane. She took out her pencil, when
it was over, and wrote on the back of a letter
the following extempore lines:

Seraphic ftrains the tender feelings move,
And Mufick melts the foul to heav'n born
    love!
Thy powers, oh Giornovich! infpire   the
    breaft,
And give the wounded mind a tranfient reft;
But, while thy notes impaffion'd bofoms pleafe,
They find the cure ftill worfe than the dif-
    eafe;
For ev'ry time thofe founds feraphic ceafe,
They leave a new invader of my peace!

She had juft finifhed the firft effort of her poe-
tical talent, which fhe intended to correct at
leifure, and was conveying haftily to her pocket, when the box door opened, and Lord
Darnley made his unexpected appearance. He

ed with infinite grace to the Miſs Fieldings, darted a contemptuous look on Mrs. Martindale (who had obtruded herſelf on the party, from a very ſlight invitation), and with more apparent pleaſure than prudence ſmiled on Lady Jane, and ſeated himſelf immediately behind her. He told her, he had been in town but a few hours; that he had firſt viſited THEIR little charge, and then called in Argyle-Street; but hearing from her ſervants that ſhe was gone to Drury-Lane, he had taken the liberty to follow her there.

Mrs Martindale who was pretending to adjuſt her handkerchief, did not loſe a word of this ſpeech; but ſaid, loud enough to be heard in the next box, That now one impediment was removed, on his lordſhip's ſide, ſhe thought the other might be eaſily accompliſhed; for ſhe was pretty ſure that young Mr, Martindale would not have much objection to ſee his name added to the liſt of happy huſbands in Doctors commons. This was too groſs an inſult to be patiently endured; but Lord Darnley, however confuſed, was too well-bred a man to recriminate. Lady Jane faintly aſked her what ſhe meant; and pleading the exceſſive heat of the houſe as an excuſe for leaving the Miſs Fieldings, requeſted Lord Darnley (who was the only gentleman in the box) to ſee her to her carriage, where ſhe inſiſted, however reluctantly, on his taking his leave.

Mr. Martindale was already in bed, and ſhe was obliged to defer ſpeaking to him till morning. Mrs. Drapery informed her, that Lord Darnley had been there, but, on finding her ladyship was out, had requested to fee her woman. That fhe went to the coach door, and he afked her many queftions about the ftate of the family ; telling her, " That he would do " handfomely by her, if fhe would keep his " fecret, which was, to tell her lady, that in " confequence of letters he had received from " town, which mentioned the difagreeable fi- " tuation into which her ladyfhip was thrown " by the machinations of Mrs. Martindale, he " was arrived, fully determined to protect her " with his life."

Oldfon, the butler, had watched this interview ; and whether jealoufy of Mrs. Drapery, or fome other fufpicion, arofe in his mind, I know not ; but he infifted on her telling him all that had paffed. Nay, he was fo refolved on knowing it, that he even threatened Mrs. Drapery to retract his promife of marriage to her, if fhe did not immediately confefs every thing to him. Any other menace Mrs. Drapery might poffibly have withftood ; but that of a difappointment in love was too powerful. She candidly acknowledged the confidence Lord Darnley had placed in her, but firft obtained a promife from Mr. Oldfon of his filence on the fubject.

He wifhed to prefuade her not to mention it to her lady ; but this trufty confidante, recollecting Lord Darnley's offer to do *honeftly by her*, longed for the moment when fhe fhould be at

I

liberty to divulge the fecret of which fhe had been till then in painful poffeffion.

Lady Jane felt a glow of fatisfaction rife on her cheek, as fhe liftened to Mrs. Drapery's information. Situate as fhe then was, every proof of regard, even from the moft indifferent perfon, became dear to her. The cruel and unmerited treatment fhe every day endured, had the fame effect on her gentle mind that a ftormy fea has on a mariner. Her heart panted for reft, for fhe faw herfelf environed by ene-mies where fhe might naturally have expected friends. She felt that matters were drawing to a crifis, that would foon determine her fu-ture fate.

The next morning fhe told Mr. Martindale of the infult that had been offered to her at the Oratorio. He feemed perfectly indifferent, and faid fhe might thank herfelf for it : that when a married woman had once openly admitted the addreffes of another man, her hufband could not be blamed for difcarding her. That he had no caufe of complaint againft Lord Darn-ley, as he conceived that he had acted only as every other gay man would do in the fame fi-tuation ; and he finifhed by telling her that fhe was perfectly at liberty to follow Lord Darn-ley's fortunes wherever they might lead her.

That calm ferenity of mind which had ever dignified the exemplary character of Lady Jane Martindale, now entirely forfook her. She uttered the moſt piercing complaints againſt her unfeeling huſband for his injuſtice and cruelty towards her, and the moſt bitter invectives a-gainſt the infamous Mrs. Martindale ; and when ſhe ſaw that it was impoſſible to perſuade him of her innocence, ſhe found it neceſſary to have recourſe to meaſures the moſt repugnant to her feelings, and at once to declare all ſhe knew : ſhe then entered into a minute detail of the intrigue that had been carried on between Mrs. Martindale and Lord Darnley at the French milliner's houſe.

Mr. Martindale rang for his hat, and went immediately to his father's, telling Lady Jane he ſhould return preſently. He did ſo ; and his countenance was inflamed by anger, as he aſked her, " How ſhe dared to aſperſe the cha-" racter of of a virtuous woman ?" She had en-" deavoured, he ſaid, to deſtroy that of Mrs. Martindale, becauſe ſhe had refuſed to become a partner in her vices. She was jealous, he ſuppoſed, of Mrs. Martindale's ſuperior beauty and qualifications, and of the attention Lord Darnley had, like other men, paid her. He adviſed her to take up her reſidence with THEIR charge, at Paddington, and limited her to three days to remove her effects from his houſe : he excepted his mother's jewels, which he inſiſted on having immediately reſtored to him. He then rang the bell, which was an-ſwered by Oldſon, whom he commanded in a peremptory manner no longer to conſider La-dy Jane as his miſtreſs, and to make known that ſuch were his injunctions to all the other

I 2

domeftics. Oldfon would have fpoken, but was prevented by a look that forbade all poffibi- lity of a reply. He then ordered a chaife and four to be immediately got in readinefs from the neareft inn, and told Oldfon to prepare to ac- company him.

The triumph of paffion was foon over; and a tear of pity. and perhaps of remaining ten- dernefs (which he ufed every effort to fup- prefs), fell down his cheeks as he took hold of Lady Jane's hand : when turning his head on the other fide, he bade her an eternal adieu. He threw bank notes on the table to the value of five hundred pounds, and then tore himfelf from her in a paroxyfm of agony that fell little fhort of her own.

IN a moment like this, how was Lady Jane Martindale to proceed ? Were I to alk a hundred people, I fhould receive a hundred different opinions ; but Lady Jane had no time for refleftion. The arrow had been aimed at her heart, and it was lodged there. She order- ed Mrs. Drapery into her prefence ; who, with many tears, befought her to compofe her- felf. She defired her to pack up in a box by themfelves, all the jewels and trinkets that old Mr. Martindale and his fon had once given to her, but of which fhe was no longer the mif- trels ; and then afked as a favour, what but two hours before fhe had a right to command, that one of the fervants might go for a hack- ney coach, that fhe might call at two or three places fhe thought neceffary, while her wo- man was packing up her clothes, as fhe defired. She was going firft to fee Mrs. Martindale ; for though her noble heart fhrunk from the idea of fupplicating her enemy, yet fhe thought it a duty fhe owed herfelf, to explain to that lady, as matters now ftood, the neceffity that had driven her to give fuch a painful explana- tion of every circumftance that could tend to corroborate her own innocence.

With swollen eyes, which she endeavoured as much as possible to conceal by her long lace veil, she stepped into the coach, and ordered it to Devonshire-Place. Alas ! the servants there had not only received orders never more to admit her, but were even insolent enough to express before the coachman their astonishment at her calling there. She then went to Miss Fielding's and had the satisfaction to find that her friend was at home. They knew nothing more of the misintelligence than what had passed at the oratorio, and entreated her to return home, and to inform them the next morning in what manner it had been settled. Lady Jane, after a short visit, returned to Argyle-Street, and found a servant of old Mr. Martindale's, who had brought a note from his son, and only waited for an answer to leave town. In it he desired her to send him an inventory, directed to Ledstone, of the things she had left there, which he said should be sent to her wherever she might appoint, as he was going to sell that estate. It contained also a request that she would quit Argyle-Street as soon as possible ; and that she would not attempt making Mrs. Drapery the companion of her flights as it would be the means of preventing that person's being respectfully settled with Oldson, and he doubted Lady Jane's future ability of recompensing her, if she attempted to prevent it.

Lady Jane possessed too much of the pride inseparable from a noble mind. to be required a third time to quit the house. She easily perceived that Drapery's views on Oldfon fu-perfeded all affection for herfelf; and that al-though he would willingly have fuffered her for the prefent to accompany her; yet he fear-ed his mafter's difpleafure were fhe to do fo.

Lady Jane defired Oldfon to change for her a fifty pounds note; fhe gave ten to Mrs. Dra-pery more than was due to her for the trouble fhe had in packing up her things, which fhe defired her to take care of till fhe fent for them. Another ten fhe gave to Oldfon to divide a-mong the fervants, befides two guineas for him-felf; and in a fit of wild defpair, unaccompani-ed by a fingle attendant, and without having tafted of the dinner that the fervants had as ufual prepared, and placed before her, fhe fent for a hackney coach at ten o'clock at night, and ordered the coachman to drive her which way he pleafed, till fhe fhould otherwife direct him.

CHAP. XXIV.

THE coachman proceeded on a journey he could not rightly comprehend, and at length stopped at the turnpike beyond Weſt-minſter-bridge. Lady Jane was ruminating whither ſhe ſhould go, when ſhe was rouſed from her reverie by a demand for the toll. Her memory brought ſeveral perſons to her recollection, but ſhe dreaded to meet with a cool reception, wherever ſhe appeared, and made known her ſtory. Of Lord Darnley's addreſs ſhe was ignorant, and the lateneſs of the hour would alone have prevented her calling on him. She deſired the coachman would drive her to Liſſon Green, where ſhe found that the family was already in bed. She knocked repeatedly, and at length with ſome diffi-culty obtained admiſſion into the nurſe's bed-chamber.

She apologized for her unſeaſonable viſit, and the myſtery of its appearance, diſcharged the coach, and lay down by the ſleeping infant. But ſhe could neither compoſe herſelf, nor let the nurſe, till ſhe had made ſome enquiries re-ſpecting Lord Darnley. The anſwer was pro-ductive of the only ſatisfaction it was at that moment in her power to receive, as ſhe found that he had promifed to be there the next morning by twelve o'clock, She foon after clofed her wearied eye-lids, and funk to momentary reft.

Lord Darnley was punctual to his appointed hour; and giving his horfe to the groom, ran eagerly up ftairs. Nothing could equal his amazement at feeing Lady Jane there, pale, difhevelled, and half-dreft, fitting with his child on her knee. She arofe as he entered, and giving mifs Darnley into the nurfe's arms, defired fhe would retire with her into the garden, while fhe fpoke to her Lord. But when fhe began to relate her mournful tale, fhe found herfelf wholly unable to proceed. She clafped her hands in fpeechlefs agony, and lifting up her eyes to *Him* who could alone fupport and ftrengthen her in the hour of affliction, fhe burft into tears.

When fhe had a little recovered herfelf, fhe explained, as well as fhe was able, her undeferved fituation; leaving the prefent difpofal of herfelf to the fuperior judgment of Lord Darnley, whofe protection was the only one fhe could now claim. He took her hand, and thanking her for the confidence with which fhe honoured him, befought her permiffion to go inftantly to town in order to provide for her a more fuitable apartment. He left her, and in lefs than three hours returned in a poftchaife, in which fhe gladly accompanied him fhe knew not, nor cared not whither.

The temporary refidence that Lord Darnley had procured for Lady Jane, was at a lodging houfe in Great Cumberland Street ; and he took one for himfelf within a few doors of it, which happened to be the fame that had been occupied by Colonel Stuart and his family. But this he did not know ; and not choofing at once to inform Lady Jane of his being fo near a neighbour, fhe alfo remained ignorant of it. Lord Darnley had called her in both houfes Lady Findlater, and faid fhe was a baronet's widow. This had been agreed on in the chaife, to prevent fufpicion or enquiry. He paffed feveral hours of the day with her, and fhe faw no other perfon. His valet, who ufually attended her, was a new one, who fortunately had not feen or heard of her before. But it was neceffary to intruft the nurfe, who was a decent woman, and to be depended on. She was moreover affured that fhe would lofe her place from the moment there was the leaft caufe to fufpect that fhe had betrayed her Lord.

From her they foon received intelligence, that fhe had been feveral times followed by different people whom fhe did not know, as fhe went in and out of town with Mifs Darnley ; in confequence of which it became neceffary to remove them, and they were fent to Brompton.

A fatality is frequently attendant on different fituations in life, which eludes all that the moft watchful vigilance can furmife to prevent it. It was fo in the prefent incident. Not all the

caution obferved both by Lady Jane and Lord
Darnley, nor the fidelity of the nurfe could
counteract the decree of fate. Great effects
proceed frequently from trivial caufes, which
can be neither forefeen nor prevented.

Lord Darnley's valet perceived that there
was fome myftery about Lady Findlater; but
being a country fellow, who knew nothing of
London, and being much confined at home, he
had no opportunity of talking over his Lord's
affairs among his fellow-fervants; and the nurfe,
who was rather a pretty girl, hardly condefcended to fpeak to him. Lord Darnley had
one morning written to Lady Jane, and intrufted as ufual the note to his fervant ; who
thought this a good opportunity to fatisfy the
curiofity of their landlady, with whom he had
frequently converfed on the fubject. She was
overjoyed at his offer, and particularly fo as he
requefted her to give it into the lady's own
hands, which was a charge he alfo had received
fiom his mafter.

She took the note, and went directly to the
door of the apartment, which was to her un-
fpeakable aftonifhment, opened by Lady Jane
Martindale, who was as much confufed as herfelf; fhe firft fufpected that it was fome trick
put upon her by her family, till fhe learned
that Lord Darnley was in poffeffion of Colonel
Stuart's former lodgings in her houfe. She entreated her to preferve the moft inviolable fecrecy, which was faithfully promifed, without
any intention of performing it·

This slender circumstance laid a lasting foundation for every subsequent event of Lady Jane's life. The moment the landlady returned home, 'she put on her hat and cloak with all possible speed, and telling the valet she was going to market, without any farther explanation, posted directly to Mr. Martindale's house in Argyle Street, whither she had once been on a visit to Mrs. Drapery, in company with Josephine, Miss Stuart's Neapolitan maid. Mrs. Drapery was at home, and in the act of writing to her dear Oldson, who was still at Ledstone with his master. As soon as she had heard ALL, she presented her visitant with a glass of her best cordial, and begged to have the HONOUR of her company another time, as she was just finishing an important letter, and feared being too late for the post. These two worthy females exchanged several polite curtesies, and parted highly satisfied with each other; the one having communicated all she knew, and the other having heard all she wished; for they were till that moment ignorant of Lady Jane's destination. Mrs. Drapery added another sheet to her already voluminous packet; and as soon as she had dispatched it, and finished her dinner, she sent for every one of the servants into the houskeeper's room, to whom she related the whole of this marvellous tale.

Mrs. Drapery was now sole mistress of the house; consequently whatever she said, was the grand rule of their actions. I must indeed except a Yorkshire groom; who having sat like

the reft open-mouthed to hear pronounced the
fentence of his lady's condemnation, declared
" he would go to her that very moment, and
know in what he could ferve her, for that fhe
was as good a lady as ever broke bread ; and
he was certain that as for Yorkfhire, there was
never a gentleman in the whole country that
would have turned fuch a tender-hearted lady
out of doors, but that he had heard thefe Lon-
doners would do any thing. He did not care
for his mafter ; he might hang him if he liked,
and keep his wages into the bargain ; but that
now he knew where to find his lady, he would
go and offer his fervice to her ; ay, and ftick
by her, if fhe would let him, without a farth-
ing wages, as long as he lived."

Mrs. Drapery expatiated on the refentment
of an enraged mafter, and the deftruction that
would inevitably overtake him, and finally prevent his ever getting another place, fhould he
perfift in fuch a foolifh fcheme :—but all would
not do ; nothing could induce Tom to relinquifh his prefent purpofe ; and with all the
blunt honefty and feeling of a TRUE YORK-
SHIREMAN, he went immediately to his mafter's ftables, where, giving up his charge of
the faddle-horfes to the coachman, he packed
up his all in a fmall bundle, and without taking
leave of his affociates, whom his heart curfed
for their cruelty, he walked with aching fteps
towards Great Cumberland Street.

In his way thither, he reflected for the firft
time of his life on what he was about. He had

K

given up his place, and all the intereſt he had, without having any juſt reaſon to ſuppoſe that Lady Jane would befriend him. What was he to do if ſhe refuſed him an afylum?—Tom had no friends in London; they were all inhabitants of Ripon; yet Tom did not repent. He already had received full compenſation for any hardſhips he might in future undergo .He had experienced that inward joy, that indeſcribable felicity of having given way to the genuine feelings of an honeſt heart. He did not ſuppoſe that his lady would ſuffer him to want; but if ſhe did, he ſhould only be reduced to temporary neceſſity, and that too in a noble cauſe; *the cauſe of injured innocence.* His friends were induſtrious, hard-working people, who would not, he was very ſure, diſmiſs him becauſe he did not bring them *Gold.* No; they had ever prayed him to remain among them ſteady to the plough, as his forefathers had been; but Tom had ſeen laced liveries in the neighbourhood of Ripon; and more from the generous motive of thinking he could henceforward add to the little wealth already poſſeſſed by his family, than any ſelf-intereſted principle of his own, he had ſet out on his perilous journey, TO ſEE THE WORLD,

CHAP. XXV.

TOM was at firſt refuſed admittance ; till by his ſobs and tears, and his aſſeveration that he had left his place for no other reaſon than to wait on his lady, he prevailed on the miſtreſs of the houſe to go up ſtairs a ſecond time, and ſhe conſented to ſee him, He briefly related by what means he had diſcovered her reſidence, and begged her ladyſhip's pardon for his boldneſs in coming after her, and the motive which had induced him to do ſo. Lady Jane thanked him for his attention, and drawing five gnineas from her purfe adviſed him to return to his place, or, if he did not chooſe that, ſhe would recommend him, ſhe ſaid, to Lord Darnley, who would procure him another. Tom looked firſt at the money, and then wiſtfully at Lady Jane ; for he feared to offend, as he begged to be excuſed taking it ; and he ventured to hint, that, not ſeeing any ſervants about her, he thought ſhe could but ill ſpare it ; and all he implored was, that ſhe would keep him in her ſervice. The poor creature pleaded ſo powerfully, that it was impoſſible ſhe could without cruelty reſiſt him ; ſo ordering him to put the money in his pocket, ſhe ſuffered him to enter on the pleaſing taſk of rendering himſelf a faithful attendant on her.

Lady Jane employed the remainder of the morning in writing a long narative of facts to her father. She endeavoured to prepare him in the moſt delicate and pathetic manner for the knowledge of her misfortunes, and anticipated the total forgetfulneſs of theſe, in his ſympathizing tenderneſs. She obſerved that ſhe had only quitted an unpleaſant home, to return to her native happy one; and ſhe requeſted his ap. probation of her joining him immediately in Ireland. With eager expectation ſhe told him ſhe ſhould wait his reply, which would in eve- thing determine her future conduct. Her hours appeared to grow lighter from the moment her letter was given to the poſtman, and ſhe fol- lowed in idea its haſty progreſs during the night; forming a thouſand pleaſing conjectures on the event of its ſucceſs. Lord Darnley had for the firſt time neglected viſiting her that e- vening; but when he called the next morning, he found her more cheerful than he had hither- to ſeen her; and as the day was remarkably fine, he propoſed their going in a hackney coach to ſee Miſs Darnley at Brompton, and walking in one of the retired paths of its neigh- bourhood. Lord Darnley returned to dinner with her, and had been juſt propoſing to ac- company her to Ireland as ſoon as ſhe received her father's anſwer; telling her, that now the Martindales knew where to find them both, he doubted not but that all poſſible means would be tried to haſten a divorce: and he hoped to receive, as ſoon as it was pronounced, her hand from her father. He had never ſpoken ſo open- ly before. In thoſe few words were compre-

hended all she wished to hear, and she felt elated at the idea of being restored to happiness.
Their conversation was interrupted by the entrance of Tom, who brought a letter that had
been put into his hands by one of the servants
from Argyle-street; it was addressed to Lady
Jane; she knew her husband's hand on the
direction, which was all he had written. In
the blank cover was a letter to himself, which
had been sent to Ledstone, and was from thence
forwarded by him.   It bore the Irish post-mark,
and was sealed with black.   Lady Jane saw the
signature, and fainted away.   Her heart fore-
boded its dreadful contents; there was no need
of her reading it, to be convinced of *this*, *her*
greatest misfortune!   Lord Darnley took it
up, and found that it contained an affecting request from the steward to Mr. Martindale, that
he would break the news of the Earl's sudden
death to Lady Jane in the tenderest manner
possible- .He had departed this but two hours
before it was written, consequently no knowledge could be had of the situation in which he
had left his affairs; but the steward added, that
as he had reason to believe his lordship had left
Mr. Martindale sole executor, he entreated
that gentleman to come with all possible haste
to Dublin.

Lady Jane soon recovered from her state of
insensibility ; but her heart was turned to woe,
and she bore this afflicting circumstance with
more composure at the moment than might have
been expected.   She looked up to Lord Darnley as HER ONLY FRIEND, for where in the

vaft univerfe could fhe claim another ?—He
fincercly felt for and pitied her, and he promifed her every afliftance, at this difmal junct-
ure, that fhe could derive from his affection,
his fociety, and advice. But fhe was deeply
affected by her recent lofs ; and her grief was
of the moft dangerous kind, as it grew into a
fettled melancholy, which increafed daily.
She continually pondered on her fituation, and
at length, without confulting Lord Darnley,
or even mentioning the circumftance to him,
fhe wrote to Mifs Fielding, giving her a cir-
cumftantial detail of all that had paffed, and
entreating to fee her. She gave Tom orders to
wait for an anfwer, and he brought back her
own letter, unfealed, in a blank cover. She
found herfelf DESPISED AND REJECTED, and a
conftant fucceffion of fad ideas filled her very
foul. The wounded mind will, like the drown-
ing man, catch at every fhadow of a fubftance;
and Lady Jane, penetrated with Lord Darnley's attentive friendfhip, infenfibly attached
herfelf to him. He could now prevail on her
with lefs difficulty to accompany him in riding,
walking, &c, till by degrees fhe gave herfelf up
irrecoverably to him, and refufed nothing to a
man whom fhe with confidence confidered as
her future hufband and natural protector.

Lady Jane and Lord Darnley were more
publickly together than formerly, but ftill kept
their refpective lodgings. In lefs than a month
after her father's death, fhe received a fecond
letter from the fteward, written at the defire
of Mr. Martindale, who was, he informed

her, arrived in Dublin to take poffeffion of all
that had been left her. He fent her word that,
on his return to England, he would fecure her
a fettlement adequate to the fortune he had
with her ; and Lord Darnley received, about
the fame time a citation from Doctors Commons.

WE will now revisit with regret our friends at allanbank ; I say with regret, becaufe we left them at the fummit of happi-nefs, and (if we accompany them at all) we muft defcend with them into the valley of woe· Colonel Stuart was furprized one morning, as he was fitting in his ftudy, by a large pack-et directed to him, which, on opening, he found to contain feveral fheets from an elder brother, who had been long fettled at Madras; and of whom he had not received any tidings for more than twenty years, a coolnefs having fubfifted fince that time between them. The Colonel was perfectly ignorant whether he was living or dead. But as old age brings reflecti-on, and draws us naturally back to our firft attachments, Mr. Stuart at laft recollected that he had a brother, who he had lately heard was not only living, but was a widower, with an only daughter. He wrote rather a kind letter to the Colonel, giving a long account of him-felf. He had been married, he faid, twice ; and had three children, none of whom furvi-ved ; and his laft wife, who was alfo his laft tie in that country, was lately dead. He com-plained of his age and infirmities, and acknow-ledged that he had made a confiderable fortune

in the eaſt, which in was his intention to be-
queath to his niece. He deſired that the Colonel would either embark in the firſt ſhip deſtined to India, or that he would ſend over ſome
perſon, in whom he could place confidence, to
attend to the ſettling of his affairs; he added,
that in caſe of his dying before ſuch a one arrived, he had already taked care to make a will
in favour of Miſs Stuart, his niece.

The Colonel exulted but little in his daughter's unexpected proſpect of future fortune. She
had enough to make her happy, and they coveted no more. Yet it was neceſſary on every
account to accede to her uncle's requeſt. She
might have a large family, and it was a duty
incumbent on him not to neglect a circumſtance
that had the appearance of turning out ſo much
to her advantage, and ſo far beyond their expectation. To caſt away a gift that was as it
were thrown into their lap, would be, according to Colonel Stuart's ideas, to render them
ſelves; unworthy the diſpenſations of provi-
dence in their favour. The only difficulty was,
to determine on who was proper to go over. It
was a long perilous voyage to be undertaken
by the Colonel; and he could not think of ſe-
parating Glencairn and his daughter, at a moment when they were on the point of marriage, and when every thing ſeemed to ſmile
propitious on their union.

When he met them, his countenance bore
the viſible marks of perturbation and anxiety;
and it was ſome time before he could collect

himfelf fufficiently to impart to them the contents of the letter. Glencairn and Mary watched each other's countenance while he was reading it ; but when the Colonel fignified his intention of firft joining their hands, and then leaving them while he made the long, long voyage, Mary at once declared that fhe would rather relinquifh every earthly advantage than fuffer her father to undertake it. To her, and to Glencairn, no increafe of fortune could bring increafe of happinefs ; and why fhould they traverfe feas to rifk the lofs of THAT, of which they were already in poffeffion ?

Glencairn ftood in a delicate fituation. His wandering heart prompted him to infift on being the deputed perfon, yet he feared two unkind conftructions that might be put on it if he did fo ; and thefe were, indifference towards Mary, and felf intereft. If either of them preponderated, it was not furely the letter. He afked Mary what he fhould do ?—She expected, yet was not immediately prepared for the queftion. It was about the time when the Indiamen were to fail ; and while Colonel Stuart retired to his ftudy to write to a friend in London in order to make proper enquiries about them, Mifs Stuart and Glencairn walked into the garden, where they agreed that there was no alternative between his going to India, and the lofs of her uncle's favour and fortune.

When Colonel Stuart faw that it was in vain to oppofe Glencairn's refolution, ftrengthened by the confent of Mary, he told him he fhould leave it entirely to himfelf, and his daughter, whether their marriage fhould take place before or after his return ; but Mifs Stuart begged to continue in her prefent fituation till he did fo. She thought fhe fhould be better able to bear his abfence as her friend, than as her hufband; they were already betrothed ; fhe could not doubt his love for her ; and fhe confidered the facrifice he was about to make, as the greateft proof that he could give of it.

The Colonel ufed all poffible difpatch in for-warding every neceffary preparation for Glen-cairn's departure ; and he foon received an an-fwer from the friend to whom he hnd written, who was one of the Eaft India Directors, in-forming him that his paffage was taken on board the Melville Caftle, which was to fail in three weeks. The arrival of this letter caufed a few pearly drops to trickle down the cheeks of Mary; but the blow was given, aud it was too late to recede.

WE will pass over the melancholy separation, and, leaving Colonel and Miss Stuart at Allanbank in better health than spirits, accompany Glencairn to London.

As he approached the gay metropolis, his mind dwelt on the idea of Lady Jane Martindale. Every carriage that he met he fancied to contain her, and every well dreft person he saw he anxioufly looked at, as fuppofing he could receive from them fome information of her. On the morning after his arrival, he waited on the Director with a letter from Colonel Stuart; but finding he was gone to Blackwall, to dine on board the Melville Caftle, he ordered a poft-chaife, and followed him. He was introduced by that gentleman to Captain Dundas and the other officers, and was much pleafed both with his acquaintance and his birth there. He was informed that the fhip was to go down the river in ten days. He returned to town with his new friend in the evening, and on their way could not forbear afking him if he was acquainted with the Martindale family?—By report only, was the reply; and indeed he faid the late tranfactions of that family were not calculated to make any perfon wifh to know more of them.

This led to an explanation, and, when they arrived, to the perufal of a newfpaper a few days old, which was at the Director's, and contained a long account of the ELOPEMENT of Lady Jane Martindale with Lord Darnley, &c. &c. &c.

Glencairn was engaged to ftay fupper, but retired to his hotel as foon as it was over; and finding that a porter kept watch all night, he put on a great coat, and walked immediately to Argyle Street. When he approached the houfe, he heard the found of fiddles, and people dancing: he at once difbelieved the report, thinking it very unlikely, if it were true, that Mr. Martindale fhould have a ball in his houfe. He was however foon convinced of his error, when he faw feveral odd-looking men reeling out of it, and heard them hallooing for coaches for the LADIES. He addreffed himfelf to the moft decent-looking one, who told him it was Mrs. Drapery's birth-day, and that all the noblemen's gentleman and ladies' women of the neighbourhood were affembled to celebrate it; that Mr. Martindale was at his county feat in Cornwall, and that Lady Jane was gone off with Lord Darnley. Glencairn thanked his informer, and returned to his apartment. He had appointed a week from that day to go on board the fhip, and was determined to employ the whole of it in making enquiries after her. He flattered himfelf that it would be in his power to " recall the wanderer home;" and fhould he fail in the attempt, it was ftill a laudable one. He thought he faw her deftitute of

L

money, and of friends; and might he not fupply the place of both?—Yet, he again reflected, was fhe deferving fuch attention from him,
and ought he not to be with-held from fhewing
it by his facred engagement to Mary Stuart?
The gentle, the virtuous, the faithful Mary
poffeffed but, alas! the fecond place in his regard; he was more rivetted by honour, than
he was bound by love.

The next morning, the Director favoured
him with a vifit, and infifted on his dining with
him. They talked of Colonel Stuart, and
Glencairn flightly touched on his engagement
with his daughter; but as feveral gentlemen
were prefent, many words did not pafs on the
fubject. Glencairn drank freely of Cape and a
variety of other wines. His life had hitherto
been one continued fcene of fobriety, and it
was not to be wondered at, in the prefent moment, that the liquor ftaggered his reafon, and
at length wholly overcame it. To this might
be added the difordered fituation of his mind,
and both threw him into a ftate of temporary
madnefs. He ftole away from the Director's
houfe, and went directly to Mr. Martindale's;
where, on enquiring for Mrs. Drapery, he
foon gained admiffion. She immediately knew
him; confirmed all he had heard; told him
where to find Lady Jane; and finifhed by faying, that had he come fooner to town, he
would have probably had the preference over
Lord Darnley.

Flufhed as he was with wine, and inflamed

by the fubject, he fcarcely gave her time to finifh the fentence, ere he directed his wayward
fteps towords Great Cumberland Street. No
fooner was the ftreet door opened, than he im-
pctuoufly rufhed forward, and, without making
any enquiry at Lady Jane's apartment, abruptly entered it. She ftarted, and was terrified
by his appearance, and received him with diftant civility. His paffion knew no bounds.
Love, jealoufy, and rage, were confpicuous in
his countenance; he called her *infamous*, and
ungrateful, and vowed to be the death of
Lord Darnley, if fhe did not inftantly confent
to go off with him. At the word *infamous*,
fhe fhuddered. Her foul difdained the menace,
and the accufer; yet fhe was ftung by his expreffions. Was that the language fhe deferved,
or had been accuftomed to?—Was there NO
difcrimination? no more gentle epithet for a
heart nearly broken by accumulated misfortunes, but which had plunged into an illegal,
though almoft uuavoidable connection?—She
had been thrown headlong down a precipice,
and was now accufed, and reproached, becaufe
fhe fell! Glencairn had not arrived time e-
nough to fnatch her from impending ruin; but
he feemed to triumph in her misfortune, and
to take an unmanly advantage of it to infult
her. She felt that her fituation laid her open
to the frowning cenfures of the world, but he
was the laft perfon that fhould remind her of
it. She had not reafon to expect to meet with
lenity from her female acquaintance, after the
KIND leffon Mifs Fielding had taught her.
Alas! were all the SEEMING virtuous charac-

ters to be unmafked, how many, more culpable in reality than Lady Jane, would be branded with the word *infamous!* The daughters of Albion, as they are the faireft productions of nature, fhould be alfo the moft generous. They fhould learn to pity, before they condemn; they fhould be merciful, as God is merciful; and they would find more favour in his fight when they wipe away the tear of anguifh, than when they wantonly and cruelly augment it. Let them not forget the old Spanifh proverb, that

Whoever throws ftones at his neighbour's windows, fhould remember his own are made of glafs.

Youth, beauty, health, and even life itfelf, are too frequently facrificed to thefe miftaken prejudices of the world. How many noble minds are overthrown by them! for I hope, and believe, that few women who are not born and educated in the path of vice, can be deemed deferving of the difgrace and opprobrium with which they are overwhelmed, from the moment they become outcafts of fociety; or, that the fufceptible mind can long fupport it! —The contempt of the VIRTUOUS, the infults of the vulgar, fanctioned as it were by their example, will not fail at laft to break a heart endued with fenfibility. How great are the forrows that arife from too delicate a fhare of it in many tranfactions of life! It has long been a difputed point, whether or not the pleafures flowing from SENSIBILITY are not more than overbalanced by the croffes, difappointments, mortifications, and infults, it daily receives from a barbarous herd of INSENSIBLE mortals. Perhaps it may be fo; yet a tender fenfible mind will ftill have pleafures, and enjoy happinefs, which thofe of a coarfer mould know nothing of. As the fource and fprings of their felicity are fecret; fo, to avoid the fneer and laugh of unfeeling creatures, they enjoy it in fecret alfo.

Hard fate of man, on whom the heavens beftow
A drop of pleafure, for a fea of woe!

LADY Jane prevailed at length on Glencairn to retire ; which however fhe was
not able to accomplifh till he had extorted
from her a promife to confider of his propofals,
and to fend him a definitive anfwer to them in
the morning. She alfo obtained his word, that
he would not take any fteps againft Lord Darnley which might interfere with her prefent ftate
of negative peace, till fhe had fome farther converfation with him. But fhe was relieved
from all apprehenfions of that kind early the
next day by a few lines fhe received from him,
in which he bade her a long adieu. He affured
her that he felt the impropriety of which he
had been guilty the preceeding evening, and
he entreated her to forgive it, as with his reafon a proper fenfe of his duty had returned ;
and that left he fhould in another moment of
involuntary inebriation be tempted to offend
her again in the fame manner, he had determined on going on board the Melville Caftle
that day ; being refolved to fulfill to the utmoft the confidence repofed in him. He would
willingly, he added, lofe his life in her defence ;
but he owed the prefent prefervation of it to
the interefts of Colonel Stuart, and his family ;
he was intrufted by them with the depofit of

their future fortune ; it was a facred engagement, which, when once fulfilled, would
leave him nothing to hope for, and nothing to
fear.

In a fhort poftfcript he added, that his deftination was to return to England as foon as he
had feen Mr. Stuart, and received his commands; when he would find out if poffible
where fhe refided, and in what fituation. He
concluded thus abrubtly, as if fearful of faying
more than he intended ; yet it was eafy to
trace his bewildered mind in every line.

Lady Jane had certainly an attachment for
Lord Darnley ; but it was rather the compulfi-
on of gratitude, than the effufion of love. She
had lately obferved in him an air of conftraint,
and fometimes of morofenefs, that fhe had not
before perceived ; yet fhe confidered it both
her duty and inclination to apprize Lord Darnley of their interview. He paufed while fhe
related it ; then feeming fuddenly to recollect
himfelf, advifed her if poffible to marry Glencairn. He did not, he faid, mean to keep up
the boyifh farce of deceiving her; but he could
not in honour to himfelf, or juftice to his
daughter, marry her himfelf. His fortune fhe
knew was not large. Yet he could fpear out
of it an annuity of one hundred pounds, which
he would fettle on her in addition to whatever
allowance might be made her by Mr. Martindale, after the divorce bill had paffed. She
muft not, he added, expect to fee him fo frequently as fhe had hitherto done; it might

prevent his forming an HONOURABLE connection, which he owed to the infancy and fituation
of his daughter.

Lady Jane liftened to this fpeech in filent a-
ftonifhment; and, when it was over, ironically thanked his lordfhip for the KINDNESS of his
intentions; but affured him that it was the laft
time fhe would degrade herfelf by feeing him.
With an air of dignity, uncontaminated by
paffion of any kind, fhe commanded him to retire, and never more to infult her either by
his prefence, or his offers of mifplaced generofity, or wound her feelings by unmerited contempt. She was at leaft his equal in point of
rank; and in fentiment, far his fuperior. She
loved the little Louifa with almoft the fame
maternal tendernefs fhe fhould have felt, had
Heaven bleffed her with a child; but her pride
had been too grofsly infulted to allow her to
give farther proofs of it. She repeated her wifh
of feeing him no more, and with haughty, but
determined refolution; forbade him to intrude
farther on her prefence. -

Lord Darnley looked abafhed, and mortified; he endeavoured to ftammer out an excufe;
but finding it would avail nothing, he made a
low bow and withdrew.

In new, and alarming affaults of fortune; if
there be leifure for reflection, the mind retires
into its citadel; and there, rejecting every ufe-
lefs or ordinary companion, admits alone thofe
rare energetic powers, whofe vigour can repel,

or vigilance elude, the fury of the storm. In such a dilemma, she naturally thought of Glencairn ; not as the future happy rival of Lord Darnley ; not as her champion, whom she might expect to find bold in his revenge of her injuries ;—but, as a friendly divinity, whose soothing pity, if it could not dissipate, would at least effuse a sympathetic balm. Yet it was not until after some struggles that she determined to write, and request seeing him once more ; and dispatched Tom with a letter to that effect, to Black-wall.

He lost no time after receiving it in obeying her summons; and drew from her full a confession of her intimacy with Lord Darnley, and his subsequent conduct. He said little in reply, but soon after excused himself on pretence of business which would detain him half an hour, and went directly to Lord Darnley's lodging, determined to demand satisfaction for the ungentlemanly and cruel treatment that he had exerted towards an unhappy and unprotected woman. His lordship having probably entertained some suspicions on that head, had paid off his lodgings, and left town an hour before Glencairn arrived there.

Cruelty and cowardice are so closely connected, as to be deemed almost inseparable. The man who would wantonly torture and destroy even the least of God's creatures, will be seldom found to possess that degree of courage which naturally belongs to the Lord of the creation, and which habitual vice only can do away.

He will tyrannize over thofe unhappy victims whom the chance of fortune has rendered fub- fervient to his power ; but he will fhrink from thofe who can reign over HIM, and ftand aghaft at the appearance of fuperior virtue. A man of real courage is a man of ftrict honour ; he will, like the tried warrior, pity, and releave as far as he is able, the lefs fortunate vanquifhed; but he will defpife the pitiful prerogative of exult- ing over, and adding to, accumulated woes. Such were the oppofite charactersof lord Darn- ley, and Glencairn.

In two days more the Melville-Caftle was to go down the river ; and Glencairn's engage- ments were of too ferious a nature to be broken. He faid nothing to Lady Jane of his knowledge of Lord Darnley's departure ; but requefted her to perfevere in not feeing him ; and advi- fed her to retire to fome more private lodging, where fhe might wait the iffue of the matter now pending in law. He told her that he ho- ped to return to England in fifteen or eighteen months ; and he begged her not to forget that fhe had one friend left, who would never defert her interefts, though the facrifice of his ever- lafting peace muft be made to the memory of her fufferings, and his own feeble condition. With thefe words he left her, but ah, in what a fitu- ation !—no friends, no fociety, not even an acquaintance to whom fhe might pour out her griefs and her mind difturbed almoft beyond the powers of reflection ! Towards evening fhe walked out, and her fteps were involuntari- ly directed towards Brompton. She would have paſſed the houſe which contained Miſs Darnley ; but by accident ſhe looked up, and ſaw her playing in her nurſe's arms, at the window. She was then about eight months old. Lady Jane could not reſiſt the temptation ; but running eagerly up ſtairs; kiſſed her with ardent affection, while the tears ſtreamed down her cheeks. The object of her walk was to find out a cheap lodging in a decent family ; in this ſhe ſoon ſucceeded, and took it from the following day.

She returned home, and was ſitting over a ſlender ſupper, rapt in melancholly ideas, when a loud knock at the ſtreet-door, and a hackney-coach ſtopping at it, arreſted her attention. Tom informed her that it was an old gentleman, who declined ſending up his name, but particularly requeſted to ſee her. She was in that ſtate of torpid inſenſibility which renders us alike indifferent to every thing, and ſhe gave orders that he ſhould be admitted. This unexpected viſitor was old Mr. Martindale ; at ſight of him her tears flowed afreſh, but he bade her be comforted. Nothing, he ſaid, that lay within HIS power ſhould be wanting to ſoften the rigour of her deſtiny. He had called to aſſure her of it ; and would repeat his viſits, though he wiſhed his family might remain ignorant of them. The ſettlement, he ſaid, of two thouſand pounds per annum that had been made on her marriage, and was to deſcend to her in caſe ſhe ſurvived her huſband, would ſtill hold good if there was no divorce, and that ſhe refuſed to ſign any bond that might be propofed to her, till fhe had been advifed how to act. His fon had been already informed by his counfel, that there did not exift any juft plea for a divorce ; and he was determined not only to apprife her of what fhe ought to do, but alfo from time to time acquaint her with what fteps were to be taken, and his opinion of them. He ftaid with her near an hour ; and promifing to call on her next evening at Brompton, took his leave of her with every appearance of pity and regard.

She received the next morning a long confolatory letter from Glencairn; but as it contained nothing more than a repetition of his friendfhip and good wifhes, we will not tranfcribe it ; but take for the prefent our leave of him, wifhing him a profperous voyage to India, and a fafe and happy return to Britain.

Mr. Martindale went as he had promifed to Brompton ; and faid he was authorifed by his fon to make known to her in what manner he chofe, that he fhould henceforwards continue to allow her one hundred pounds per annum ; and that he had given orders to his banker to pay her immediately five hundred pounds, as a prefent from himfelf. She had hitherto thought of, and now cared, fo little about pecuniary matters, that fhe was perfectly fatisfied with his propofal to execute a deed of feparation, that fhould preclude the poffibility of her debts falling on her hufband. This was agreed on, and figned by both parties the following day, and every thing appeared to be terminated to

the fatisfaction of all thofe who were concerned
in it.

C H A P. XXIX.

F R O M the time of Glencairn's departure,
Mifs Stuart's health began to relapfe into
its former ftate of declining ftrength. Fre-
quent faintings, lofs of appetite ,and a total de-
jection of fpirits, were the alarming fore-run-
ners of what was foon confirmed to be a rapid
decline. The Colonel and herfelf received feveral letters from him, and in the laft, dated
from the Downs, he took his long farewell.
But thefe, inftead of affuaging her grief at his
lofs, vifibly augmented it. She perceived a
chilly referve in his manner of addreffing her,
that was inconfiftent fhe thought with the nature of their engagement ; and his filence refpecting Lady Jane Martindale (an account of
whom they had feen in the papers) was to Mary the fureft proof of his not being indifferent
about it. In a few weeks Mr. Courtenay became their vifitor ; but knowing the fituation
of her heart, he dropped all pretenfions to be
her lover, and gloried but in the title of her
fincere and fympathizing friend. He divided
with the Colonel his attentions to her ; and
his naturally cheerful difpofition often forced a
fmile from her pale and placid countenance,
M

while it feconded the anxious wifhes of her venerable father, by fometimes enabling him to
affume an air of gaiety from which his heart was
very far removed.

Many months paffed in which their hours
were thus uniformly, and not unpleafingly divided.   The Colonel and Mr. Courtenay generally rode out ; and when the cold was not
too fevere (for it was now winter) Mifs Stuart frequently accompanied them behind a fervant, for fhe was too weak to venture alone on
horfe-back.   They had one morning in the
month of December extended their ride beyond
its ufual bounds, when they were overtaken
by a fudden ftorm.   The hailftones pelted them
with fury, and thick flakes of fnow fell in a-
bundance over them.   They found themfelves
nine miles from Allanbank, and were obliged
to take fhelter in a fmall cottage, till they could
difpatch their attendant to the neareft town
where a chaife might be procured, and which
was at a much greater diftance.   They did not
reach home till near feven o'clock in the evening, and the ftorm had not yet abated.

They had but juft changed their wet clothes,
and were fitting round the blazing fire, waiting their early fupper, when *Keeper*, the faithful houfe-dog, announced by his loud barking,
the unufual appproach of vifitors.   He was
foon echoed by feveral other dogs, whofe
peaceful flumbers he had difturbed, as they lay
ftretched round the comfortable hearth of the
hofpitable parlour.   The rain pattered againft

the windows, and the wind loud whiftled through
the trees, which hardly fuffered them to diftin-
guifh the rattling of carriage wheels, till it approached clofe to the outward gate. Mary's
heart firft bounded high with fluttering expectation, and then funk with dire difmay.

The inhabitants of Allanbank foon affembled at
the door; from whence, after a fhort interval
of painful fufpence, they could perceive, by the
glimmering light of the different candles they
held, a female form, which, lightly tripping
up the lawn, was enquiring of every one fhe
faw, whether Mifs Stuart was there? On being anfwered in the affirmative, fhe flew to her
embrace, and, without giving Mary time to
recollect herfelf, afked her if fhe had quite forgotten her old friend, Sophia Beaumont?

Mary drew back with fear, as thinking fhe
beheld her ghoft; for how could mother St.
Etienne, a confirmed nun of one of the ftricteft
orders in France, be not only liberated from
her confinement, but alfo a folitary wanderer
in a remote part of a kingdom to which fhe was
an entire ftranger? A moment's paufe convinced her; and that moment drew a tear of
blood from her heart, as it brought to her remembrance the fituation of *perfecuted France!*
that country in which fhe had paffed fome of the
happieft hours of unconfcious infancy; where
fhe had fo often witneffed the gay dance, the
feftive board, the jocund fong, and all the
fprightly attributes of light-footed felicity.
Alas! how fad, how bitter, how fudden,

M 2

how heart-breaking, was now the vaft Reverfe!

Mary welcomed her friend with unfeigned
fatisfaction, and when fupper was over, Mifs
Beaumont began her pathetic narration. She
dwelt with pity on the violation of every facred
inftitution. The Catholic religion, whofe outward forms pourtrayed the excefs of romantic
fuperftition, now ftood unmafked, and terrible
to view. The favage chiefs of France, whofe
hands were perpetually employed in fhedding
without mercy the blood of innocents, had laid
low the buildings that were devoted to the fervice of God, and at length dared to deny his
name. Nor did fhe forget (while the tear of
pity ftreamed down her cheeks, and down
thofe of her auditors) the holy fifterhood of
her now violated, but once facred, afylum.
Thofe aged and venerable nuns, whofe life had
been fpent within its quiet walls, and who,
devoted fince childhood to their religion, had
peaceably and uniformly fulfilled its duties,
were now torn by the rough hand of violence
from their folitary cells, and expofed to buffet
with the ftorms of a world they had never feen,
and of which they had coveted only A GRAVE!

The great clock ftruck twelve; and, by re-
minding them of the latenefs of the hour, re-
leafed the compaffionate hearts under the roof
at Allanbank from dwelling farther on the melancholy tale; and Mifs Beaumont, fatigued
by her long journey, was glad to retire as foon
as fhe had fatisfied them of the means which
brought her thither. An Englifh family to

whom she was unknown had conducted her by
the way of Oftend to London, and fupplied her
with money more than fufficient to defray her
expences to Scotland. This charming girl,
though French by birth, was calculated to a-
dorn human nature ; her heart recoiled at the
horrors exercifed by her ferocious countrymen,
horrors fo great they want a name, and beggar
all defcription !

IT would be difficult to meet with minds more perfectly congenial than were thofe of Mary Stuart and Sophia Beaumont. They were charmed with the fociety of each other, yet Mifs Beaumont's delicacy was wounded by her being wholly dependent on her friends. From this motive fhe wifhed, after a few months refidence at Allanbank, to remove from it till fuch time as fhe might be able to withdraw her flender fortune out of the hands of her family. She was an adept at all kinds of needle-work, and thought it might be practicable for her to gain a maintenance at Edinburgh; but Mifs Stuart's precarious ftate of health would not permit her to hint at it. She was every day fomewhat weaker than the former one; yet with that flattering hope which is almoft conftantly attendant on her fatal diforder, fhe derived the moft fanguine expectations of her recovery with the approaching fpring. Mifs Beaumont and Mr. Courtenay were indefatigably attentive to her; but the Colonel was too well aware of her danger, not to ftand himfelf in need of that affiftance he endeavoured to give his dying daughter.

Let ftoicks enjoy their frigid infenfibility,

and philofophers boaſt the command of paſſions they never felt ; but where is the heart endued with NATURAL TENDERNESS, that could have refrained ſympathizing with Miſs Beaumont in her feelings for her friend ?—Courtenay's could not. His admiration of her amiable difpofition, which was ſo feelingly difplayed on this melancholy occafion, led him by degrees to a more tender ſentiment, which he had ſome reaſon to think did not remain long unnoticed by the lovely Sophia.

It was an union that Miſs Stuart ardently wiſhed ; and the deep bluſhes which had once overſpread Miſs Beaumont's face on hearing his name inadvertently mentioned, confirmed her in the opinion ſhe had formed of their mutual attachment. I have already faid that Mr. Courtenay poſſeſſed a confiderable fortune in Ireland ; but his generous foul diſdained the idea of hoarding money, and it was not unuſual for him to exceed the bounds of his income by deeds of charity and benevolence. He was at this time about fifty years of age ; and had rambled ſufficiently about the world, to wiſh to be at length quietly fettled in it. He had partly determined on going to Ireland for that purpoſe, when he ſaw Miſs Beaumont. His paſſion for Miſs Stuart had worn away in proportion as his hopes of being united to her diminiſhed.

Miſs Stuart ſent for him one morning into her dreſſing-room ; and taking from a drawer a miniature of herſelf that had been donc in Italy (and which, contrary to her expectation, Glencairn had not asked for at his departure), presented it to him. She requested that he would give it to Miss Beaumont; adding, that she was greatly mistaken in her conjectures if she did not receive it with additional satisfaction from his hands.

This speech was too flattering to the wishes of Mr. Courtenay, to be misunderstood by him. His next care, after giving the picture as desired, was to open his mind to Colonel Stuart, and to repeat to him what had passed. The young ladies had already come to an explanation on the subject; and before evening it was resolved on, with the hearty concurrence of all parties, that Mr. Courtenay should receive the hand of Sophia.

In less than three weeks he had made an honourable settlement on his fair intended; and soon after, the marriage was solemnized. Miss Stuart insisted on being present at the ceremony, but fainted before it was over, and was with difficulty conveyed from the church to her chamber. Her heart rejoiced at the happiness of her friend: but it brought sad recollections to her mind, and was near subduing the little strength that was left her. Mr. Courtenay hired a small house that was fortunately vacant in the neighbourhood of Allanbank, as they were determined not to leave Miss Stuart till the curtain of death had been gently drawn over the last scene of her existence.

They had been fettled there about ten
months, and Mrs. Courtenay's fituation was
fuch as to require every' precaution and care
that a fond hufband, and anxious friend, could
beftow on it, when it unfortunately happened
that fhe was one evening fitting with Mifs
Stuart in. her apartment, and the London
newfpapers arrived. Mrs. Courtenay opened
them, and began to read ; but had not proceeded far, when fhe faw the words Melville Caftle.
Eager to fatisfy her own impatience, and that
of her unhappy friend, fhe began to go through
the paragraph ; but ftopped in the middle of it,
gave a loud fcream, and fell in hyfterics on the
floor. Her cries foon brought the fervants up
ftairs, who were followed by the Colonel and
Mr. Courtenay. The fatal nryftery was inftantly revealed ; the alarming paragraph ftated that the Melville Caftle was arrived fafe at
Madras ; but that a boat belonging to her had
funk at the entrance of the harbour, and that
all the perfons on board had unfortunately perifhed.

Mifs Stuart difplayed the moft heroic fortitude on this occafion ; her fears for her friend
fuperfeded every felfifh pang, and fhe feemed
to foar above mortality. She fhed no tears,
but fweetly fmiled as Mrs. Courtenay recovered, and even endeavoured to perfuade them
that fhe had a prefentiment of Glencairn's not
being of the number of thofe unhappy paffengers. A premature delivery, and the death of
her child, were the only ill confequences that
befel Mrs. Courtenay ; and which, by detain-

ing her at Allanbank, was not unaccompanied
by confolation to Mifs Stuart, who was too ill
to vifit at her houfe, and derived her greateft
comfort on attending her, in a room adjoining
to her own. Mrs. Courtenay foon recovered ;
but it was to witnefs a fcene which, though
fhe had long expected, fhe was ill prepared for.
Mifs Stuart found herfelf one day fo much
better, that fhe requefted they would all indulge
her by dining in her room. She had drefied
herfelf to receive, as fhe faid, her vifitors,
with unufual care. When dinner was over, fhe
defired Mr. Courtenay to lead her to the piano-
forte ; when faintly touching the difcordant
ftrings, fhe endeavoured to go through her favourite air,

I know that my Redeemer liveth,

which fhe attempted to accompany with her
voice ; but her ftrength failed in the attempt,
and fhe funk motionlefs on the chair. When
fhe came to herfelf, fhe affectingly took a hand
of her father's, and repeatedly preffed it to her
lips. She then for the firft time acknowledged
to them all, that fhe was fenfible of her approaching diffolution. She begged the Colonel
would comply with her request, and, in cafe
of Glencairn's returning to England, that he
would make him his heir ; faying, fhe could
not die in peace unlefs fhe obtained the promife
of that which lay neareft to her heart. In half-
broken fentences he affured her of it, and bade
her be comforted.

Towards evening fhe begged of Mr. Courtenay to read prayers to her, and defired that all
the fervants might be called up ftairs to join in
the pious fcene. Soon after they were over,
fhe called Mr. and Mrs. Courtenay, and the
Colonel, round her chair; and embraced the
two former as fhe prayed of God to blefs them.
But when her father drew near; when fhe felt
his arms clinging round her waift, as if to
fhield her from the tyrant who was advancing
with hafty fteps to feparate them for ever, fhe
faintly articulated the word *farewell ;* her head
funk on his bofom, and with a deep and heavy
figh *fhe expired !*

It was fome time before they could perfuade
themfelves fhe was dead; a faint glow tinged
her cheek, and a fweet fmile was vifible on her
countenance, from the moment the feparation
of the foul and body had taken place. They
laid her gently on the bed, and applied a mir-
ror to her lips. But the faithful moniter refufed to deceive. Her breath was fled; and her
foul, already towering beyond the confines of
mortality, was reaping the reward of innocence and virtue.

C H A P. XXXI.

MR S. Courtenay refigned to her hufband the melancholy office of confoling the afflicted Colonel, who vainly endeavoured to reconcile himfelf to the fad feparation. He however derived comfort from the idea that it could not be of long duration, for he felt that he fhould not long furvive his Mary. He took a mournful pleafure in decorating her fenfelefs corfe with fuch flowers as his humble green-houfe could fupply. He watched the fad proceffion as it moved from the houfe ; at the head of it, was the faithful M'Kenzie, bending her pallied frame towards the earth in fpeechlefs woe. Mr. Courtenay fupported her ; nor did his manly countenance lofe fight of its dignity while overfpread with the tears of affection and fympathy. Eight young Highland girls bore the precious burden to its deftined home ; and the folemn fcene was conducted with that filent awe which intermingles itfelf with pious refig- nation to the infcrutable will of Heaven.

The ceremony over, the mourners return- ed ; and by degrees, Mr. and Mrs. Courtenay left Colonel Stuart's houfe to inhabit once more their own. Yet they continued as one family, and omitted nothing that could tend towards alleviating the diftreffes of their venerable friend. But this care was not long allotted them. In a few weeks, Colonel Stuart entreated them to give up their houfe, and to take poffeffion of Allanbank ; confidering it as their depofit till, by the unavoidable arrangement of his affairs, it might hereafter become neceffary, through Glencairn's return, for them to relinquifh it.

He foon after made his will, and difpofed of every thing as his daughter had directed ; allotting only fome trifling legacies to Mr. and Mrs. Courtenay ; a fmall but fufficient annuity to Mrs. M'Kenzie; and remembrances to his other domeftics in proportion to their age and fervices. He farther ftipulated, that in cafe of Glencairn's death without iffue, his whole property was to devolve to Mrs. Courtenay, and HER heirs for ever. The bufinefs of life being finally fettled, the excellent Colonel Stuart refigned his breath, while glorifying his Redeemer that had heard his prayer, and was going to reftore him to his Mary.

Mr. and Mrs. Courtenay remained in quiet poffeffion of Allanbank. Exemplary patterns of domeftic felicity, they had already paffed three years there ; during which Heaven bleffed them with two children ; nor did they know a day's feparation, till Mr. Courtenay went to Ireland for fix weeks, on bufinefs relative to his own affairs. His amiable Sophia refufed all fociety but that of her children and the worthy M'Kenzie ; who being now too old to interfere

N

in household management, was become her constant companion. They could not hear of Glencairn, though they had used every endeavour to know his fate, on the return of the Melville Castle. All they could discover, was, that he was not of the number of the drowned paffengers in the boat. They had landed him at Madras; and from their not having received any tidings of him since, they concluded that he was either removed to some more diftant part of India, or died soon after his arrival there. But they did not appropriate any part of his intended fortune to their own use ; they ftudiously endeavoured to accumulate, and enjoyed the pleafing, difinterefted hope, that still exifted, of his return to the full enjoyment of it.

Let us now revert to the ill-treated Lady Jane Martindale ; who, hurried progreffively from one falfe ftep to another, found many Lord Darnleys, but few friends. Old Martindale frequently vifited her ; but fhocking to relate ! foon convinced her, by his propofals, of the depravity of his mind. He told her that her future fortune was in his hands, and that he would provide for, or forfake her, according to her treatment of him. He queftioned her as to the ftate of her prefent finances; and on finding that her thoughtlefs extravagance had reduced them to the lowest ebb, he threw a fifty pound not on the table, and endeavoured to extort from horror and fear, a facrifice that in a generous breaft muft be ever facred to love alone.

Fallen as fhe already was in her own efteem, and in that of others, fhe yet could not hear a fentiment fo degrading to humanity, without feeling a mixture of terror and furprife. Though reduced to the laft exigences, fhe would fain have returned the note to its defpicable owner: but he infifted on leaving it ; and, fhewing evident fymptoms of difappointment and confufion, foon after took his leave.

Lady Jane gave herfelf up a prey to inward defpair, and outward diffipation. While the tears rofe in crimfon torrents from her heart, fhe wildly decorated her perfon with the infignies of joy ; and fought a tranfitory relief in falfe pleafures, while fhe continued to be a ftranger to every real one. The doors that fheltered virtue, were clofely barred againft her approach ; thofe of vice, only, ftood upon to receive her. In every new lover, fhe fought a friend ; in every new lover, fhe gained an enemy. She had heard of Mifs Stuart's death, but to Glencairn's fate fhe was wholly indifferent. Several weeks elapfed without her hearing any thing more of old Mr. Martindale; and fo invincible was her prefent averfion to him, that although from motives of prudence fhe was with-held from publickly expofing him, fhe rejoiced at her deliverance from the fight of fo unworthy, fo unprincipled a relation.

She was one day waited on by an elderly gentleman, whofe appearance prejudiced her warmly in his favour. He fpoke the language of pity, and of friendly advice; founds to which she had been long unaccustomed. After the necessary introduction, he informed her that Mr. Martindale, senior, died suddenly two days before, in an apoplectic fit, and that his will had been that morning read. a codicil was found to have been lately added to it, by which he ratified to Lady Jane the enjoyment of the two thousand pounds per annum, in case of her surviving her husband ; but that he had not bequeathed her, for temporary supplies, any legacy whatever.

Lady Jane cared so little about worldly concerns, that she heard of this disappointment without the least discomposure. Her mind had now yielded to that state of hurried perplexity, that did not allow her time to reflect on all the miseries attending her hapless situation. She had taken an elegant house in town; and its expences were unceasingly defrayed by the divers successors to her attention. All intercourse between her and the little Louisa Darnley had been long since prohibited by the unfeeling lord ; who, callous to misfortunes of which he had been a principle author, now wantonly regarded her, wherever he met her, with the piercing look of ineffable contempt. The affection she once bore him was totally obliterated ; and she could meet him and Miss Fielding together, which was not unusual. beholding them with the same degree of contempt which they did not fail manifesting towards her upon every occasion.

A black coach, and all the outward trappings
of woe, were the tokens by which fhe foon
defcried Mrs. Martindale ; who daily paraded
the Park and Bond-ftreet with all the folemnity
of DECENT widowhood. To this was oppofed
the gaudy equipage of Lady Darnley, late
Mifs Fielding ; but this did not excite in the
breaft of Lady Jane, one fenfation of forrow,
envy, or furprife. Her feelings were however powerfully affected by a premeditated infult
fhe received from Lady Darnley, a few days
after her marriage ; who having ftopped her
carriage one morning at a fhop in Bond-ftreet,
was fpeaking to one of the people at the coach
door, when Lady Jane paffed by. Mifs Darnley was with her, and eagerly called to Lady
Jane ; when Lady Darnley fuddenly drew the
fpring blind, to prevent her enjoying the flender fatisfaction of even looking at her.

C H A P. XXXII.

MRS. Martindale did not long remain a widow. Ere the long twelvemonth was expired, during which it was neceſſary for her to ſubmit to the doleful attire, and to put up with a corner of one of her drawing room windows being darkened by a hatchment, ſhe made a promiſe that when once the happy peri- od arrived, ſhe would beſtow her hand on a more ſuitable lover than ſhe had found in her old man. Captain O'Trigger, whoſe commiſ- ſion centered in a daſhing cockade, had paraded his ponies about the city of Bath during ſeveral ſeaſons. But, though the gaming tables were in general propitious to him, the choſen ſocie- ties were not ſo. The miſſes all vowed, that Captain O'Trigger was the fineſt fellow in Bath ; but the mammas and guardians gave him ſo little encouragement, that the Captain at length thought it beſt to beat a precipitate retreat, and try his ſucceſs in London. He was a fine, tall, handſome looking man ; neat, but prepoſterous in his dreſs, and fond to a de- gree of his perſon. No man knew better than himſelf the names of all the different eſſences and pomatums imported from India and France. From the powerful otto of roſes, down to the more reviving, but more humble-lavender wa-

ter, his dreſſing-room was the repoſitory of
them all; which, together with his ponies, a
few fans from Italy, and ſome pots of rouge
warranted vegetable (the two latter articles he
reſerved for the happy fair on whom he might
hereafter fix his choice,) compoſed the whole
ſtock in trade of this FASHIONABLE MILITARY
HERO.

Captain O'Trigger, whoſe modeſty was not
in the habit of laying any embargo on his inclinations, no ſooner beheld our young widow,
and was informed who ſhe was, than he determined to lay cloſe ſiege to her ; and as an ad-
vantageous marriage was the firſt grand object
of his purſuit, he was reſolved to transform his
character into exactly any one that he might
find on father enquiry would be moſt likely to
determine her in his favour.

He began to try the whole battery of his ar-
tillery againſt the vain Mrs. Martindale; firſt,
by the aid of a ſmall glaſs, ſuſpended to a black
ribbon, and dangling from his neck ; with
which he aſſailed her wherever ſhe went ;
while the expreſſion of *a damned fine woman !*
was uttered JUST loud enough to catch her
ear. At firſt ſhe thought his accents favoured
rather too much of the brogue ; but at length
cuſtom reconciled her to him, and ſhe hazarded
not ere long to avow a diſtinguiſhed preference
to Captain O'Trigger over the reſt of his com-
petitors,

He ſoon became the acknowledged intended

of the beautiful widow; not that she cared for him in her heart, but her vanity was gratified, at the idea of mortifying her rivals, whom her opinion had magnified into a much greater number than even Captain O'Trigger himself could lay reasonably any claim to.

The last few weeks of Mrs. Martindale's funeral appearance were dedicated to preparations for her approaching nuptials; on the strength of which, her favourite Captain was enabled to cut a much greater figure than before. A sumptuous vis à-vis was building at Hatchett's, by his exprefs order; and in which his taste shone conspicuous. She was perfectly convinced of the sincere attachment of this *Knight of Industry*, and in giving him her hand, bestowed on him also her own house in Devonshire-place; and every appendage of luxury she parted with in his favour, with as little difficulty as she herself had formerly obtained them.

For some months the torch of Hymen blazed with unremitting ardour; but the instability of human happiness soon overpowered, and at length wholly extinguished it. Mrs. Martindale (now Mrs. O'Trigger) was fatally convinced that she was the dupe of a designing fortune-hunter; for such in reality was her chosen mate.

It would be needless to detail the many occurrences which led to the sad reverse of fortune she was henceforward fated to undergo.

Her hufband's extravagance manifefted itfelf at
the gaming-tables, and elfewhere. Her money fheltered him from a goal, but its fource
was not inexhauftible; and fhe had no fooner
deprived herfelf of every future comfort, for
his prefervation, than he left her to lament her
error in obfcurity and poverty. Captain
O'Trigger, after felling her houfe and all fhe
was poffeft of, at length wholly deferted her ;
and the only account fhe ever after received of
him was that of his having returned to a former wife in Ireland, with whom he had fled to
fome diftant clime, far beyond the reach of law,
juftice, honour, or humanity.

Lady Jane Martindale continued for a time
to run the giddy round of thoughtlefs diffipation ; but her heart, that had ever unwillingly
yielded to its dictates, was foon tired of its tranfient gratifications, and fighed after the humble fcenes of peaceful retirement. · But thefe,
alas ! were no longer within the boundary of
her own acquifition. She had no friend to fupport her tottering fteps ; no foothing hand was
ftretched forth to yield her comfort ; no confolatory parental voice remained to welcome her
out of the path of vice. She was, as it were,
left alone in the vaft univerfe ; the fmall falary
allotted her by Mr. Martindale fhe duly received ; and hitherto temporary additions to it
from her acquaintance had not failed her ; but
fhe knew thefe could not laft long, and fhe had
acquired experience enough to teach her that
they would exift no longer than fhe was inclin-

ed to facrifice her happinefs to the enjoyment of them.

In this fituation, fhe had already continued fome years, anxious to exchange it, yet not poffeffing refolution enough to effect it, when fhe was one morning furprifed by the appearance of Glencairn. He was fo much altered in perfon, that fhe had at firft fome difficulty to recollect him; but his heart was the fame. He had already been in Scotland, where he had taken poffeffion of Colonel Stuart's eftate; ftill infifting, that Mr. and Mrs. Courtenay fhould not quit Allanbank. His voyage to India had not been profperous. Mr. Stuart's affairs were, when he arrived there, in fo deranged a fituation, that, at his death, which happened foon afterwards, they were found to be little worth the trouble that had been taken on their account; and he was at length obliged to abandon them, after having obtained but a very flender advantage in favour of his friend and patron. But the refidue of Colonel Stuart's fortune was yet more than fufficient to anfwer any purpofe of his own. He had liberality of fentiment fufficient to make every allowance in favour of Lady Jane Martindale's miftaken conduct; and while he could yet entertain the hope of making her happy, the praife, or the cenfure of an ill-judging world were to him equally indifferent.

He prevailed on her to accompany him to Edinburgh, where fhe foon convinced him that the genuine uprightnefs of her heart had

remained uncontaminated by *fashionable levity.*
Nor was she long there, before, by her admiſſion into a reſpectable family, and the delicate
caution obſerved by Glencairn in his viſits to
her, ſhe gained that countenance and reſpect
which had been wrenched from her in England
by the iron hand of cruelty, injuſtice, and op-
preſſion. Not a year had paſſed after this happy tranſition, before the death of Mr. Martindale, by liberating her from the moſt ſacred,
and moſt abuſed of engagements, enabled her
to beſtow her hand, and large encreaſe of fortune, on him who had ſo nobly deſerved them.
The amiable Mrs. Courtenay ſhone forth on
this occaſion the bright repreſentative of spot-
less virtue. She knew how to pity thoſe errors ſhe had never known ; and thoſe tempta-
tions which, as ſhe ſweetly, ſaid, ſhe might
not have been able to have withſtood, had fate
dealt by her with the ſame ſeverity it had done
towards Lady Jane Martindale. The pomp of
widowhood would have been but ill diſplayed
by that hitherto unfortunate lady. She neither
affected the weeds of ſorrow, nor the trophies
of joy ; but with all the decorum due to herſelf, and to thoſe with whom ſhe was now ſo
happily connected ſhe ſurrendered, as ſoon as
decency would permit, the name of *Martindale*,
and became entitled to the more happy one of
Glencairn.

In a ſhort time Mr. and Mrs. Courtenay inſiſted on putting them into poſſeſſion of Allanbank, and themſelves retired to their eſtate in
Ireland. Glencairn gloried in the ſucceſs of

his unſhaken fidelity. Lady Jane proved herſelf the woman of honor and gratitude, by the
conſtant rectitude and unremitting care of her
conduct ; nor was Glencairn leſs remarkable as
a huſband, than he had hitherto been from his
ſteady attachment as a lover, to the *object of
his firſt choice.*

Mrs. O'Trigger plunged into exceſs of wan-
ton depravity ; and a refuſal of Lady Jane's
propoſal to receive and protect her at Allanbank was the only inſtance of denial ſhe experienced from her indulgent huſband. His
acquieſcence to pecuniary offers was not however with-held from her, while any hope remained of her deſerving ſuch an act of kindneſs;
but her life was at length wholly abſorbed by
drunkenneſs and debauchery ; and the premature end of it was well calculated to afford a
ſtriking example to A BAD HEART !

Nothing was wanting to augment the felicity of Glencairn, but an encreaſe of his family ;
and even that was almoſt compenſated by the
recollection that Mr. and Mrs. Courtenay
were his heirs.

We will now take leave of Lady Jane Glencairn, and her happy huſband. Conſtant patterns of connubial happineſs, their lives were
ſpent in the exerciſe of every ſocial virtue ;
and Lady Jane proved the happy *Contraſt* between *unavoidable error and premeditated vice.*

THE END.

www.ingramcontent.com/pod-product-compliance
Lightning Source LLC
Chambersburg PA
CBHW021121020726
47500CB00003B/870